"Here I am!"

shouted the desert, loud with life, for life there still was in it, waiting, stored, like seed. "Here I am. Did you forget me? Forget me despite your dreams of me, your dreams of the sun and the rain and the antique tribes who roamed me once with their herds and their weird ways? You, who moaned and whined, covering metal-tape with cries and yearning, you, you effete thalldrap. Now's your chance to prove you can do more than sit on your tail complaining and drinking sapphire wine with your tears of self-pity. Come, come and do battle with me, come and fight me. I'm more than a match for you. I'll devour you if I can, but I'll do it cleanly and openly, not with words and dark little tanks in Limbo. Don't be afraid of human death and human age. I've seen it all, and I know it. It's just dust blown over the rocks. Look at me, how dead and old I seem, and yet, watch me grow, watch me live. Come on. Come and find me. I'm waiting."

Tanith Lee

DRINKING SAPPHIRE WINE

DAW BOOKS, INC.
Donald A. Wollheim, Publisher

1633 Broadway, New York, N.Y. 10019

FIRST PRINTING, JANUARY 1977

3 4 5 6 7 8 9

 DAW TRADEMARK REGISTERED
U.S. PAT. OFF. MARCA
REGISTRADA. HECHO EN U.S.A.

PRINTED IN U.S.A.

TRANSCRIBER'S NOTE

Although I have put the Four BEE into equivalent modern English, the Jang slang vocabulary which the writer uses pales in translation. I have therefore left the twenty or so odd words she/he employs untouched, and included a glossary, which provides an adequate if imperfect guide to what they mean An additional glossary has also been added at the end of the book with reference to city and Jang customs and some other oddities, not explained in this second part of the autobiography.

Glossary of Jang Slang

attlevey	Hello.
dalika	Violent argument.
derisann	Lovely, beautiful.
droad	Bored out of one's mind.
drumdik	Utterly horrible, the most ghastly thing.
farathoom	Bloody, fucking hell.
floop	Cunt. See also *thalldrap*.
graks	Balls.
groshing	Fabulous, marvelous.
insumatt	Unsurpassable.
onk	Mild ejaculation, e.g., "Bother."
ooma	Darling, honey.
ooma-kasma	Extreme term of affection, e.g., "love of my life," not generally used.
promok	Moron.
selt	Slow on the uptake, easy to fool.
soolka	Well-groomed. Applied by Jang only to non-Jang.
thalldrap	See *floop*.
tosky	Neurotic.
Vixaxn	A word never written in full in the previous section of the autobiography. Though spelled fully here, the meaning—though obviously still pretty bad—is also still obscure.
zaradann	Insane, nuts.

Glossary of General Terms

Glar	Early Four BEE title, similar to professor. The term hung on as a polite name for Q-R teachers at the hypno-schools, but otherwise was extinct by this time.
mid-*vrek*	Middle period of any *vrek*, lasting forty units.
rorl	Four BEE equivalent of a century.
split	Four BEE minute.
unit	Four BEE day.
vrek	Period of one hundred units.

Part One

1

"Hergal," I said, "if you say that one more time I am personally going to knock you straight through that wall."

Hergal looked at me in grave wonderment.

"All right," he complied, and said it. He didn't look surprised, either, when I got up and did exactly what I'd promised I'd do. Maybe he was only humoring me. As he lay there on the other side of the wall, surrounded by bits of shattered silk-of-crystal, I added:

"I suppose you're too much of a damned ignoramus to know what comes next?"

"Absolutely," said Hergal, removing glittering chips from his long orange hair and wringing spilled orange wine from his sleeves.

"Swords at dawn," I said, "or pistols. Take your pick. My challenge, so it's your choice."

"You *have* been at the History Records again," remarked Hergal, "and as I observed prior to our little *dalika* just now, being a male half the time is getting you all tangled up, old *ooma*. You're predominantly female, so why don't you—" No chance to finish. I laid him flat on his back again.

He stared up at me woefully.

"Swords?" I inquired. "Or pistols?"

"*Graks*," said Hergal. "If you want to play ancient grandeur, do it in the Adventure Palace like everyone else."

And thus, rising to our gold-shod feet, we glared momentarily eye to eye, after which he strode out into the morning, whistling one of the current Jang favorites: "I only want to have love with you, for you are so *derisann*."

About twenty robots and Q-Rs, of various descriptions but unanimously unfriendly, were bearing down on me, so I also strode out of the little restaurant on Crystal Terrace and made off along Crystal Walkway in the opposite direction to my friend, mate, and crony, Hergal the Turd.

To be quite frank, what really tied me up in a knot was the pure logic of Hergal's deductions. True, I had been at the History Records—again. True, I, predominantly female as I was, had been male with no break for almost three *vreks*. There had, of course, been a variety of assorted bodies, but they were all much the same.

There were many like Zirk, who, when a male, tended to rangy heroic types with shoulders the width of Committee Hall doors, rippling bronze musculature, and a loud persona —for which Zirk made up, when female, by being about three feet tall, delicate as porcelain, and timid as a Four BOO sand-rabbit. Then there were the ones like Kley, who, when male, was a quiet, well-mannered nonentity, and became a raging bully when in girl-shape. I, however, remained much the same either way. Always inclined to violence, chivalry, and general moodiness, the size of my breasts, or any alternative apparatus I happened to have about me, didn't really color the situation to any vast degree—at least, I don't think so. But my particular circle, which had enlarged itself, as most Jang circles do, over the last twelve *vreks*, had got sensitive about my "eternal maleness"—as Hergal was pleased to call it. I had come to the conclusion that Hergal, himself predominantly male, resented my intrusion on his preserves. He and I got on well enough when I was female and he male. But I had noticed, as time slithered by, that when we were both of one ilk, the fur flew. Another thing that troubled male Hergal in the male me was perhaps my superior success with the female portion of the group.

Thinta, in fact, was becoming a bit of a pain.

"You need looking after," she would say. "Someone to keep an eye on you. You remember that business before. I haven't forgotten. Neither has the Committee, you can be sure of that." And then, glowing her cat's eyes at me, "We'll get married for mid-*vrek*, and you can come and live at home with me, and everything will be *groshing*."

Thinta's home was another of the ubiquitous palaces of Four BEE, with seven emerald towers, each one packed floor to roof with pale-green cats. Thinta had always had a cat fixation, which, unit by unit, seemed to be getting worse. Open a door in her place and a cat fell out; lie down on a couch in her place and a cat jumped on you. Having love there with Thinta could be an ordeal. The first time, I thought it was Thinta wailing and making those long, white-hot, silver-wire runnels down my back. But it wasn't Thinta, it was three of Thinta's cats.

"No thanks, Thinta," I said. "We can marry for a unit, yes. But we'll go to the floaters."

But Thinta still liked to keep an eye on me. She would signal me in the center of night, and wake me out of deep slumber, and ask:

"How are you?"

She would arrive in her safe pink bird-plane at all the least convenient hours of sunlight, and say:

"Are you *sure?*"

Meanwhile, Zirk, when a sand-rabbit, timorously appeared at the tables of restaurants where I was eating, or on the surface of water-skating pools, and whispered flutteringly:

"Why, *attlevey, ooma. Fancy* meeting *you!*"

And Mirri, Hergal's last love, the one he added to our circle personally, and with whom he spent so many secret hours, now pursued me up and down the movi-rails, walkways, and sky-lanes of Four BEE, her hair flapping like a rainbow flag, and her face alight with predatory instincts. Even Hergal I vaguely recall arriving at midnight in female form, and saying in a fascinated calculating fashion:

"You know, I think I begin to understand you at last."

The scene with Hergal, however, in Crystal Air, had come about because we'd heard Danor was moving back from Four BAA.

Danor and I. That was distant history.

Danor and I and that silly chilly sequence those many *vreks* before, when she told me—he then, I she—that he couldn't have love and like it. Danor jumping from a window in the floater clouds, and falling hundreds of feet into the city—pointless action, since the robots would be on him and have him removed to a new body inside the hour—yet just as if he *meant* it. . . . To me, now, that event was somehow the beginning of what happened to me, all those things that happened to me back there, twelve *vreks* in my own past. My fight against the world, the biting and snapping of a wild animal at the sun. Look over my shoulder, and I'd see, in the wreckage, the struggle to find a challenge, the wild attempt to make a child and the fatal mistake that killed that child in its crystallize twilight; the nutty relationship—the only relationship that held anything for me—my love and my rapport with that pet I never named until it was too late. My pet who died. Death, death everywhere, death in this society where no one *dies*. . . .

"I wonder what sex Danor is going to be for the homecoming," said Hergal, looking at me obliquely through his apricot lashes.

"Female," I said.

"Yes, she did stick at that for quite a while," said Hergal.

Maybe he'd guessed why—because she said it was easier to pretend to passion that way. Lucky she never read the History Records as I had done, and found, among their other little horrors, the ironic essay on frigidity, some ten *rorls* old.

"Still," said Hergal, "she's been in BAA long enough to get over her perpetual girlhood. That'll leave just you and Hatta as the circle freaks."

I resented, I'll admit, being classed with Hatta, whom we'd just seen bundle by outside, looking like a scarlet balloon on three legs that had been struck simultaneously by lightning and plague. Hatta had also thrown knives in my heart, but that was way back with the rest. Now he seemed to go about his compulsive ugliness in a spirit of inventive venom that was almost engaging. Each body was worse than the last, which should have been impossible. Maybe he hoped that we'd both throw up fourth meal at the sight of him when he leered in at the crystal window.

"Seen Mirri lately?" I asked Hergal casually. I, too, had an armament.

"With you, I saw her," said Hergal, "but don't reckon on making Danor. Danor cracked up when you cracked up, and got out of BEE to get away from you. That's why this is the first time she's been back since."

"How flattering," I said, "to have such a profound effect."

"Listen," said Hergal, "you sit up there on your tail in the History Tower, in the dust with a couple of rusty robots that don't know what *rorl* it is. You read about things that don't exist any more and won't ever exist any more. Adventures, wars, illness, obsolete social behavior patterns—*poets*." This last was a knock at my appearance, modeled by me from a sort of amalgam of the romantic pale young men who, with masses of loosely curling dark hair, slight and graceful builds, aquilinity of feature, and large shadow-smudged blue opals for eyes, were conjured three-dimensionally on the history walls from long-ago drawings of a vanished intellectual world. All these beings traditionally died young—of ancient, unheard-of diseases of the lungs, at sea, in battles, in burning planes and unexpected accidents. It seemed required of them, and I won't say I never laughed in their pretty and tragic faces. Death of that kind was a hard thing to realize, even for me, in this place where death never permanently threatened human life. Imagine those poets' expressions, rescued by the robots of Four BEE, and emerging newly clothed in flesh from the Limbo Tub. "Do you mean I have to write more verses of my bloody poem after all? How utterly *drumdik*."

"Listen," reiterated Hergal slyly, "you haven't had a body change for ages. Go to Limbo and have one, and I'll meet you. Do you remember that body of yours with the cinnamon skin and the lemon hair? That was really *insumatt*."

"You mean the female body?"

"Oh, yes," said Hergal. "Why not get them to look it up and order it again? Then you and I can make a couple of units of it."

"So you know for certain," I said, "that Danor is coming back female." Hergal looked at me. I added: "Danor and I have a longstanding agreement. I shouldn't like to let her down. Perhaps you could persuade Mirri. I'll tell her I've got something else on."

"You only get them," said Hergal, "because you're still seven-eighths one of them. It's cannibalism."

"What erudition," I said. "Can it be you've been to the History Tower too? With so much time on your hands these days . . ."

"You're a misfit," said Hergal. "You always were. You don't go to the Dream Rooms because you can't even get through a dream any more without messing it up. You're trying to live eighty *rorls* back in the past because you can't come to terms with things as they are."

"You can," I said. "You've stopped crashing onto the Zeefahr Monument, and last mid-*vrek* you hanged yourself in Ilex Park off a jade tree, where all the kids from hypnoschool could see you. How well-adjusted."

"At least," said Hergal, "when I get out of Jang I'll be able to make a little kid to *go* to hypno-school, since I didn't manage to annihilate the last one."

Definitely he had been snuffling about in the History Tower. The words were archaic, as half of mine were now. But no matter. This was the moment when I swatted him right through the wall, and we presently parted company.

I'd known, however, despite my challenge, that he was a safe dead loss for a duel, even if he had read about them. Picture Hergal firing from the shoulder at ten paces in the dawn. Yawning would spoil his aim.

2

"*Attlevey*," said a sharp metallic voice. I detected who it was before I looked round.

"Well, if it isn't Kley," I said.

Kley was female right now, which meant watch out, but, when I glanced about, in a new body. Dazzling. Hair like lava, eyes like raw gold, skin like polished brass, and dressed to kill in see-through patterned with gold daggers, and with a brazen skull—of all antique masterpieces—grinning on her groin shield.

"I must say," she must said, "you're looking pale."

"That's the idea, Kley. My body's designed to look pale."

"Oh, yes. You're being a consummated poet, aren't you?"

"Consumptive, *ooma*, consumptive," I said.

"Filthy," she said. "Your ideas are absolutely sick."

"Sick as anything," I agreed. "Sick as three Jang in an angelfood factory."

"And your vocabulary!" she bawled. "Those *words!* Factory? What's *that?*"

"A place where they make audio plugs," I said.

We were on the old, non-moving walkway that trails up from behind Third Sector Committee Hall, and leads eventually to the History Tower. It was a remote route, not much favored, for the Tower itself was rarely visited, and so Kley's arrival on my heels was as unexpected as it was unwelcome.

"You ought to pull yourself together," she now bellowed, her voice striking and bouncing back off the steel statues lining the walk. "It's all over the city about your *dalika* with Hergal. Even the flashes reported it."

"Whoopee," I said. I had turned and was walking on, but she kept after me and even grasped my arm firmly with a gold-gloved hand.

"Danor's coming back on the sky-boat at sunset."

"Yes, I know."

"And you're going to meet her?"

15

"Kley," I said, "right now I'm on my way to the History Tower."

"Oh no," she said, "you're coming with me. I've been reading the latest Jang love manual, the *Purple Summit*. You're going to marry me for the afternoon and we're going to do everything it says together, including the Trapezium with the red-hot Star-Whip, and—"

"Kley," I said, "look at me. Do I look strong enough to go through anything like that?"

"Of course you don't," she snapped. "That's how you had the body made, isn't it? But if I know you—"

"Kley," I said, "you don't."

Unlike the bright and burnished History Museum—where a couple of *rorls* worth of Flash Records and similar junk were kept—the History Tower, Harbinger of the Arcane, was suitably black, old, grim, and uninviting.

And the facade worked pretty well. How many people went there? Twice, when I was pouring over some vis-plates, I heard the distant puttering of somebody else in another part of the building, the hiss of a flying floor going up and down. And once an Older Person, female and disapproving, came marching in to look up the origins of some committee motto for a treatise she was writing—or said she was. I wasn't in my poetic body then, and she scowled at me as I slouched there robustly. I heard her later mutter something to one of the elderly robots that clanked about the Tower that Jang should not be allowed in.

And when did I first enter those portals? About twenty units after I got out of Limbo that time, twelve *vreks* gone, when I made history myself by passing out cold, and was compulsorily refitted with flesh. Thinta had visited me, oh yes, I well recall. Thinta, clothed by innuendo: "Do you remember that funny word . . ." I had uttered it, apparently, on my way down. The funny word had turned out to be "God." Thinta said she'd looked it up in the History Records. She said it sounded like a kind of very large special computer. She said it worried her, so she'd come along and worried me with it so she could feel better. In the end I arrived at the Tower to investigate for myself. I never really unraveled the mystery. The farther back you went, the more fragmentary the Records—and it was something to do, I believe, with the days when uncertainty was everywhere. However, I began to like the privacy of the Tower, and I began to delve into the

Records, fragmentary or not, for their own sake. The things they teach you at hypno-school are barely a scratch on the surface.

It was a substitute, too, let's face it, for the activities I'd given up, like the Dream Rooms, since even the most meticulously programmed dreams—awash with swords, dragons, and so on—invariably turned into nightmares of the unprogrammed sort. The very last time I went I woke up screaming, and created history once again in Four BEE. I'd dreamed I was fighting a great monster of fire that burned flesh from bone, and it wouldn't die however often I severed its head or pierced its heart. That was a dream I'd grown used to since, but at least I didn't pay a Dream Room any more to saddle me with it.

In the Tower, a crotchety robot came wheezing up. It looked quite pleased to see me, and its lights did a little display. The rooms smelled of metal and dust and a sort of incense smell, too, from some of the very ancient books which were kept in special vacuum containers and turned over by air jets rather than machine, to keep them from crumbling into bits.

Actually I didn't delve much on this particular visit. I sat in my alcove with some old (about ten *rorls*) music playing at me, and began to entertain rather romantic thoughts about Danor. Of course, she might be the disappointment of the *vrek*. Or she might have turned into a Hatta-horror, though it seemed unlikely. Poor frigid Danor. My reading up here had given me a few ideas. Looked at calmly, Danor was in the nature of a scientific experiment, but dress yourself in a poet's skin and you find you've reached for a machine, and started to compose poetry to go with it. A Jang love poem for Danor, as elegant, charming, and empty as an unfilled room.

She must have left Four BEE about the same moment I emerged from Limbo, carrying a cask of metal tape under my arm—that depressing saga of events I'd authored there. Possibly Hergal's mouthings were true; she'd fled in fear of me, since our individual descents into misery occurred about jointly. But why come back?

Finally I switched off the music and abandoned the alcove. Beyond the transparalyzed windows, the Four BEE sun was trudging down the sky.

And there, on a steel bench, lolled Kley, smoking a hilarious golden cigar.

"Paler than ever," she remarked acidly. She flipped open

an armband and offered me an energy pill, which I declined. "Going to faint at Danor's feet, are you?"

Yes, someone would always dig that up.

"That shouldn't be necessary," I said.

"Well, come on," she vociferated. Her finger-long nails flashed in the sunset. "The whole circle's going to the lock to welcome her in. Probably a a few other circles, too, recollecting that old thing she had about playing hard to get."

"Go on, Kley," I said. "Strain yourself; play hard to get."

She nearly got me with a sideswipe of those nails, and five robots came over and hustled us out with disapproving creaks.

3

Bells rang. A soft explosion marked the closing of the dome locks, and Danor's sky-boat sailed down out of Four BEE's turgidly perfect sunset like a large silver bird.

You could tell the boat came from BAA, city of the fabulous. Rubies flashed on the covered window spaces, which protected the passengers, as ever, from glimpses of the wild desert that reigns and rampages about beyond the domes. And when the exit ports opened, they spilled a crowd in trailing cloaks of noncombustible fire and similar finery, and with alarming android pet animals and crates of extraordinary luggage, not to mention a flock of baas, now bees. No longer did I use a bee. I carried things about on my person when I bothered to carry anything. The old bee, which always fell on me, more than partly with my own connivance, now lay among that heap of forgotten detritus that cluttered the upper rooms of home.

Horgal was loitering at the edge of the Arrival Stretch with Zirk-as-hero. Both gave me sidelong apprehensive looks, and Zirk flexed a bicep or two in obvious warning. Of Hatta there was, fortunately, no sign, and Mirri had not come either. Thinta, however, materializing in a mild frenzy, darted up and glared at Kley with one of those unique Thinta-glares that convey as much menace as a lollipop.

"Attlevey," said Kley, poking me in the ribs by way of a comma. "She here yet? Or do I finally say *'he'?"*

"Are you all right?" Thinta asked me. "You look so washed-*out*. (Danor? No, at least, we don't know.) Did you remember to have a meal injection?"

Nobody knew what body Danor was going to be in. Zirk was having a bet with a Jang male from some other circle that it was that nice little thing in pink, and the Jang male— Doval, by name—was saying he thought it was the other, nicer little thing in red.

"Yes, Thinta," I said.

19

"But are you sure?" Thinta persisted. "Because I've brought some nutrition pills with me in case."

Just then I saw Danor. It was quite easy to spot her—yes, her. The dashing quality and the poignancy were still there, and you could see them clearly, shining up like light through colored glass. If you really looked. The others were still jostling and haggling and waving at the four points of the compass. And Kley suddenly yelled out that maybe Danor had graduated to Older Person status, and slapped on the back a dignified woman, who promptly began to complain about it to the nearest robot. Amid the confusion I slipped my guards —Kley, Thinta—strolled across to the reception area, and reached it at the very split Danor came away.

Hair like a blue raincloud, and a BAA dress of transparent lightnings. She was leading by a chain of sapphires a sort of swan animal, elegantly stepping on very stiff legs, its plumage just the shade of her own lavender eyes.

"Hallo, Danor."

She glanced up and at me, quizzically.

"You know me? How *derisann*. And you?"

I told her.

"Oh—" she said, as if she were going on to say something else, and then hesitated. But her eyes, those lavender eyes, were open as two doors on a sort of turmoil—alarm, pleasure, cowardice, memory. She'd gone right back to the time she/ he jumped off the floater, I could tell, right back to the Secret. No one else knew, surely? No one but me.

"You sealed my lips with a kiss, remember?" I said.

"Did I? Oh, yes," she said. Then a troubled frown. She had apparently progressed beyond that kiss now, beyond the Archaeological Expedition, to the part when I, uttering incomprehensible moans about God and boredom, fell prone upon the floor of the Robotics Museum. Returning afterward from Limbo, I had found her gone, or would have had I been thinking of Danor then. "Are you happy?" she said to me, blatantly, gently.

"I'm noted for it," I said. She looked away. "And you? How was BAA all these *vreks?*"

"*Insumatt*," she said, "of course."

Her swan meanwhile had lifted one stiff immaculate leg and was peeing up the side of a reception pillar, a thing which surprised me, since the android animals of BAA are generally without bodily functions. Two Q-Rs were spraying disinfectant over all of us except, maybe, missing the swan.

Zirk had come bounding up too, and was staring nonplussed at the scene, his Herculean face going magenta with explosive emotion. Finally he got out:

"You must be Danor!"

"Danor?" I said. "This isn't Danor. Danor is the nice little thing in pink."

Danor remained silent.

Zirk floundered and his pectorals deflated uncertainly.

"Well, I did reckon the one in pink was . . . But then, who's this?"

"Does it matter?" I said. "You look after your interests and I'll take care of mine." I craned to his ear. "After all, I gave up the Danor idea when I saw you and Hergal getting to work. I should watch Hergal," I added.

Zirk spun round, registered Hergal's position, and then galloped boatward to envelope the pink girl with Four BEE gallantry. How surprised she was going to be. Kley and Thinta were gawping at me, and Kley's golden eyes had a leopardine gleam.

"Danor," I said, "there is a robot bird-plane for hire about ten paces to our left. You didn't protest a moment ago, so I assume you won't now." And I took her hand, and she, I, and the swan ran for the plane and leaped inside. The swan landed on the dashboard, its beak making a merry rattling sound and its wings smiting left and right. I depressed the "PAY ON LANDING" button, closed the ignition switch, and we were sailing into the velvet upper air of the city. The swan also erupted into flight and whizzed about our heads.

Danor giggled, hauling on the sapphire chain. The swan settled abruptly and the bird-plane plunged to port.

"How silly," said Danor. "Be calm," she murmured to the swan, and to me: "It was a genetic mistake. The flashes in BAA reported it. It came out of the tank wrong and they were going to dismantle it. But I asked Kam if I couldn't have it, and he said yes and arranged it."

"How splendid of Kam," I said.

"Kam was an Older Person," said Danor. She folded her hands in her lap on top of the swan. Very serenely she said: "We lived together for eight *vreks*. Yes, *ooma*, a Jang girl with an older male. Watch the buttons," she said softly as I inadvertently spun us into a Hergal-type dive—the old Hergal. "The Committee finally got around to suggesting we part company. They told us, very kindly, that it was not done, not good for us, not healthy. They told Kam that he was ruining my life, so he made me go."

The swan began to sing in a high-pitched inappropriate voice:

"I only want to have love with you, for you are so *derisann*."

We changed to a bubble, and got along Peridot Waterway and so home. I didn't pay for the bird-plane—I seldom did when I could avoid it—but I felt I had to for the bubble, since the swan, obviously a creature of irregular habits, crapped lethargically all over it. Danor did not apologize for the swan, for which I admired her.

At home, we went into the suite of rooms I still occasionally used. An immediate machine came crawling out of the wall and sidled up to Danor, imploring her to let it get her some topaz meringue or crushed fire-apple. Danor declined, which intrigued me; once she had adored food at any hour of night or day. She inquired instead if the swan could have some syntho fruit juice. I acquiesced with mixed feelings.

We sat together in the garden by the pool under the huge artificial stars of Four BEE—Danor, the swan, and I.

"Can it swim at all?" I asked.

"Oh, no," said Danor. The swan was apparently a total failure, which was why she loved it.

We had said no more about Kam. At least, I had asked nothing and Danor had volunteered no more. But now, reflectively, she began to talk again. I could tell from her voice, so level and unbitter, that the story caused her great pain, but it was a pain she had mastered. She was informing me, not because she needed to, but out of a sense of fairness. Because to her, as to me, the brief weird trouble between us in the past had achieved importance over the *vreks* which followed. Danor and I had never been close. In those days Hergal was nearer to me, even Thinta, in her irritating way. But now, under the monotonous starlight, we might have been the offspring of the same makers, brother and sister.

"When I went to BAA," she said, "I was male again for a little while. A couple of other-circle Jang had followed me; I did it to shake them off, and it worked. One unit I met this older male in the Weather Gardens—you know the place in BAA where they have special weather effects, thunderstorms and snow and everything. I was with a crowd watching an avalanche—they only lay it on twice a unit and it was rather impressive. Then this male came up to me, and he said reproachfully: 'If you were going to be here, why didn't you signal me?' I said I didn't know what he meant. Then he stared very hard, and he blushed. How often do people blush? It was sort of unusual and rather attractive. He'd designed himself very handsomely, and he didn't have that pompous, anti-Jang look either. He said: 'I am sorry. I thought you were my child. He's predominantly male, and his last body did look very like yours. But how stupid of me. What must you think.' I said I thought it was quite natural, and I didn't mind, and was he the guardian? He gave a little smile, the sort of smile that isn't really a smile. 'No, the other maker is his guardian. I don't often see either of them.' By this time the avalanche was finished. When he had looked at it, his eyes were really far away, unfocused. He didn't seem happy or enthusiastic. Have you noticed, *ooma*, I expect you have, how nearly everyone is always happy and enthusiastic, and rushing about, and laughing and screaming? He was very restful, and I suppose he thought I was restful, because we were both very silent and sad-eyed. Presently he said he was called Kam, and would I care for a glass of opal wine or some Joyousness or something. Just then I think he wanted to make believe I was his child and I'd come to visit him. It eased out, bit by bit, how he and the other maker didn't get along well now, and the other maker, predominantly female, had insisted she be guardian to the child, and it rather seemed she might have turned him against Kam. Kam didn't actually say this. He was trying to be impartial, simply because he felt angry about it, and knew he might not be. I liked him. I said I wished he were *my* maker, I hadn't seen my two since hypno-school ended.

"That was the start of it. We began to go about on a maker-child basis. I was still male then. He was so very nice to me. He paid for everything, and he took me to see the sights —things I hadn't even heard of. And he introduced me to his friends, though most of them were fairly anti as usual, and even had me meet a Jang circle or two, the children of his contemporaries. One day there were these two gorgeous Jang girls in his palace. They'd seen me and liked me, apparently, and Kam had encouraged them. He came in, being jolly and maker-ish. He expected I'd want to get married to one of them for the unit, but of course I didn't. And it wasn't just the old thing—the having—love thing—either. It made me realize. When I didn't bite, the two girls eventually flounced out. I told Kam I was predominantly female, and due for a change. He looked slightly taken aback. He looked something else, too—nervous, and not only that, somehow glad. I knew then, and I think he did. I went to Limbo that night. He didn't go with me. This was the body I came out with. I wouldn't change it now, and if I had to, I'd replicate —fortunately that's a successful fashion that you started, *ooma*. I ordered it in these soft colors because I'd seen he liked them. His home was all blues and mauves like evening skies. Am I making him sound *floopy, ooma?* He wasn't. But he was very kind. I came back at dawn, and I wondered if he was still asleep. But he'd been up the whole night. He was walking about on the roof, and he saw me and came down. To begin with, I felt scared, he seemed so flabbergasted. He just stared at me. And then he apologized and mumbled something about you never knew with Jang, I might have turned up the shade of a fireball, with a knife on each hip. I simply took his hand. I didn't know what I wanted, really. I wasn't analyzing or being rational, and I wasn't afraid. I didn't even remember the idea that Jang never have liaisons with older people. I mean, they never do, do they? I suppose, maybe, it must have happened once or twice, but only for a unit, and all hushed up and hidden afterward, with everyone ashamed and rushing off to suicide or something.

"He said, 'Darling, I'm at least half a *rorl* older than you, and you know I can't follow Jang custom and marry you— there's no provision for older people to marry. You do realize that?' I said, 'Doesn't matter.' He looked troubled, for me, because I was a Jang and breaking the unwritten law—though probably it *is* written, too. So I kissed him. I hadn't planned to. I'd resigned myself anyway, ages before, that having love, for me, was a nonevent and always would be. You see, I hadn't imagined it would be any different with him. I just wanted to make him happy, because he was so special to me. I was ready to play and pretend anything." Danor's eyes sparkled. Sublimely, majestically, she made a particularly unequivocal Jang sexual gesture. "Well, well, *wasn't* I due for a surprise?"

"Yes," I said, "I'd had a couple of ideas about that too."

I tried not to sound sullen. Kam had stolen my thunder, but never mind, at least her story was original.

"All that marrying business," Danor said, glinting. "All that delay. Part of me always knew I'm spontaneous. He taught me that. Oh, *ooma*," she said suddenly, the light fading from her face, "I loved him. Do you understand what I mean?"

"Yes, I know about love," I said. "Like God, it doesn't seem to function any more."

"They won't let it function. Do you know what happened? One night his child arrived—how ironical. He was a sort of amber male with cold eyes. He took one look at me and ran off to his guardian, and about three splits later there was a messenger baa in the house from the Committee. They spoke to both of us, together and individually. They were very kind, that was what made it so silly. They explained that the age and experience difference simply wouldn't work. That Kam was a maker-figure for me and I was a child-figure for him. I said, what did it matter if we were happy? But they convinced Kam, and that unit he said I must go. He was very firm. He ordered me out, and his eyes were full of tears."

I glanced at her. She was still calm, wholly in command of herself. She looked very beautiful, very desirable in the cool starlight, which, despite its artificial idiocy, is effective. But what can you do with a friend who sits grieving stoically by your pool for a lost lover that isn't you?

Just then, the swan tottered—probably drunk on its syntho-juice to the water's edge, and tumbled in.

I had a moment's wild hope it would regain a lost instinct and begin to swim, but it sank like a stone, only its beak protruding for an instant, honking out a snatch of song—"You are the wonderful sun of my sky!"—which was presumably the only way it could cry for help.

I suspect the swan had reminded me somewhat of the pet, though the pet's intelligence had been razor-sharp, for all its *zaradannity*, while the swan was manifestly a mental deficient.

Not stopping to calculate, I plunged straight into the pool after the bloody thing, and swiftly emerged with its struggling, wet-feather body, which I deposited on the bank, against great opposition from the swan itself. It promptly puked the water it had swallowed into half the silk-flowers and then sat down on the other half with a look of mild self-congratulation.

I rose from the pool, my poet's gear of black cactus-velvet plastered to my skin, and my loosely curling hair matted to a consistency guaranteed to shred my skull when next I came to brush it.

Danor had begun to cry, almost unobtrusively.

"Poor swan," she whispered, but I knew who she meant.

I knelt by her and, regardless of my saturated condition, she clung to me. I was familiar with this scene, had acted in it with myself as Danor. I held her close, and presently picked her up and carried her inside. At the door I paused to tie up the swan and send some house machines with towels and things to look after it. Danor thanked me between her sobs.

I set her on the larger, goldwork couch.

"We haven't married," she said flatly. "Jang tradition."

"*Vixaxn* Jang tradition," I said quietly, and her mouth was tearfully laughing as I found it.

4

Danor lay sleeping like an azure dream, but outside in the sunny garden the swan, having snapped its leash, was plodding about and sneezing like a vivacious klaxon. Though it was the pop-pop of the porch signal which had waked me.

I switched on the signal image.

There stood a three-dimensional of Zirk, flexing and unflexing his deltoids grimly, and almost purple in the face.

"*Attlevey*, Zirk," I cheerfully greeted him.

"*Attlevey!*" roared Zirk. "*Attlevey!* You lying, double-crossing, maladjusted *thalldrap!* You regurgitated, *tosky*, maker-making *promok!* You—"

"*Attlevey* again, Zirk. Let's start all over, shall we? What do you want?"

"You've got Danor," Zirk accused.

"Danor's here, yes."

"So it *was* a filthy trick, deliberately perpetrated. The whole circle standing there like fools, howling at the wrong female 'Welcome, Danor!' And you'd dragged her off. And she's been here the entire night, and you never married. Listen," he growled, "Jang get cut out of circles for doing half of what you've done."

"Piss off, Zirk," I cordially invited him, and flipped the recluse switch.

Outside, the swan had sneezed down a couple of miniature copper arbors, and seemed set for the pool again. I went out and got it and brought it in. A machine bustled from under the bed and tied up the swan, and gave it a plate of something, who knows what, but it tucked into it with enthusiasm. Danor had waked. She looked as though she might have heard my chat with Zirk, but she only said:

"Do you think we should signal anyone, Hergal or Kley? Or Thinta?"

"I have a feeling we won't need to," I said.

However, it was Hatta who communicated next, though not from the porch.

27

Danor and I were in the bathing unit, not precisely bathing. Some houseproud machine or other, trying to anticipate my needs, had deactivated the recluse switch. Heralded only by the signal light, scarlet, balloonlike Hatta materialized in our midst.

"Er," said Hatta. Maybe he flushed, no one could tell. The image winked out, but around thirty splits later, at a more appropriate moment, he reappeared.

"Sorry," said Hatta. He cleared his throat and said, "Hello, Danor."

"*Attlevey*, Hatta," said Danor. "How are you?"

"Oh, mustn't grumble," said Hatta.

"Why not?" I demanded. "Looking as you do, I'd say you have every right."

He peered at me sorrowfully.

"You haven't been very ethical," he said, "and to involve Danor—"

"I involved myself," said Danor.

"They want you out of the circle."

"Splendid," I said. "And don't expect any tears."

"Zirk's been going to the History Tower," said Hatta carefully to me. "Did you know? He's been there all night. You recall that foolish joke you had with Hergal—about a dwull."

"A what? A *duel?*"

"Duel, then. Yes. Well. I think Zirk's been looking them up."

Close by, the swan sneezed. Hatta blinked uneasily.

"Don't say that," he warned. "It's no laughing matter."

I met Zirk outside Silver Mountain two units later. Danor was inside, buying some pet vitamins for the swan, and a pet-maintenance Q-R was giving it an injection to stop it sneezing. Zirk came up behind me, tapped me on the shoulder, and, when I turned around, knocked me about six blocks down the street. I don't really remember it particularly. I woke up flat on my back, or nearly, since some unknown Jang girl had cradled my head on her lap. The sky was full of robot planes in midswoop, thinking someone had suicided as people were always doing every second of the day. A small crowd had gathered, as usual when anything vaguely out of the ordinary occurs, and Zirk stood, arms akimbo, grinning his great white teeth.

"OK," he announced, "I've challenged you. Are you going to accept?"

The Jang girl gazed down at me over her glamorous breasts, and stroked my brow.

"There, there," she soothed.

I smiled at her, but Zirk shouted:

"Don't you waste a split on him. He's going to be cut up and cut out in that order. He's had love with half the circle without marrying them."

The Jang girl looked shocked. So did the crowd, and the robots milling from the planes. I got up and my head rang, and I staggered, but no one helped me this time.

"Well, do you accept?"

I'd cottoned on to the general idea by then.

"All right, loudmouth, I accept."

Zirk beamed. I might have known the History Records would have a worse effect on him than on me. He was all thick-brained swashbuckle and teeth.

"I'll mince you," he promised. "Do you accept swords?"

People round about, mostly the Older Ones, asked each other what "swords" were. Some of the Jang knew from their Dream Room fantasies and the Adventure Palace.

"Been practicing?" I inquired.

"Do you accept swords?" he grated.

"If it will shut you up."

Zirk looked about at the crowd, and flexed everything he had.

"Since my body is a good foot taller than yours," he said, "I'm willing to permit you to get a new one on a larger scale."

"Gosh, *thanks*," I drooled.

"The time is tomorrow at dawn, Ilex Park, west corner."

I could see the crowd making a mental note. We should attract quite an audience.

Just then Danor and the swan came out of Silver Mountain. The swan had stopped sneezing but, judging from the disinfectant aroma, it had done a few other things instead.

Danor halted when she saw the gathering.

Zirk bowed to her, bulging.

"Everybody understands," he said penetratingly, "that none of this was your fault. I've no quarrel with *you*, Danor. In fact . . ." He coyly winked, then spun on his heel and rolled off.

The unneeded robot planes were scurrying skyward, but a couple of Flash Center bees were homing in, so I took

Danor's hand and began to walk her and the swan quickly away.

"It's happened at last," she said, very low.

"It certainly did. I bet the flashes will be blazing with it tonight."

"Have a body change," she said. "Come back a female. Then he won't have the gall to fight you."

"What does it matter?" I said. "It's my fault for starting it off with Hergal. And in any case, if he shoves his crackpot pseudo-steel fencing foil right through me, the Limbo Tub will have me back on my feet in no time, right?"

"But, *ooma*," she began, "don't you see—"

"Yes," I said.

I saw. If Zirk really meant what he said, and melodramatically stabbed me to the heart, it would be the first intended murder committed on our planet for over sixty *rorls*.

5

Somewhere about then, I made a decision. I decided that if Zirk and I were really going to that sort of limit—a killing —he was going to have to kill *me*. The decision was rational, which was rather a joke, since I have always been an emotional and impulsive character. I can think in straight lines, but, when it comes to the point, I find myself running about in circles, as usual. However, the thing with Zirk was that if anyone received the label "murderer," it wasn't going to be me. Zirk had, after all, so far led a fairly blameless Jang career—an excess of suicides and body changes, a measure of dome sabotage, and a nervous breakdown or two—but these were all perfectly normal as far as the Committee was concerned. I, on the other hand . . . Oh no, I wasn't taking any chances.

Yet there was something working against me, something I'd never have reckoned on.

I'd forgotten that, ever since that last compulsory body change twelve *vreks* before which followed the historic swooning, I hadn't suicide once. In itself this was fairly untypical, particularly since formerly I'd been one of the worst offenders, constantly drowning in order to acquire a new exterior. But suicide had become unappealing to me after that traumatic time; now I waited the prescribed thirty units between each change, and anyway, hardly ever did change. What was this? Could it be that I, even in the safe cities, had acquired an antique and obsolete fear of death? Or was it rather, perhaps, that somehow, somewhere along the stony path of my pathetic Janghood, I had evolved, despite everything, a *life*-wish?

And for the record also, for about a *vrek* I had been indulging in fencing practice, off and on, at the Adventure Palace. Presumably Zirk had taken a course, too, but really, built as he was, a power axe was far better suited to his style than a poetic slender sword, weapon of emaciated princes and dreamers.

31

Dawn takes place always at the same split each day, prophesied always by the same streamers of rose and ember, and the identical singing of mechanical, light-reactive birds, dumped here and there in the parks and gardens. Imported real birds from BOO ignore dome-dawn with lofty disdain, and, having witnessed an authentic desert sunrise or two, I don't blame them.

The jade leaves of the jade-trees of Ilex Park glowed and flashed under the pink sky. Long, black-green shadows were creeping down the slopes, and a little artificial ground mist—most artistic—was smoking about in the grottoes and groves.

As I approached the west corner, however, I began to hear the hubbub.

I won't say my heart sank. It had been fairly sunk for hours, what with the depression that had set in at the thought of letting that moron Zirk impale me. But a cryogenic sensation idled up my guts like a cold snake out for a walk. Of course, odds on there would be a crowd, after Zirk's public fashion of announcing our plans. This, though, sounded as if half the city had crammed itself into the park, and I wasn't in the mood for making a spectacle of myself in front of forty million sensation-seeking *thalldraps*.

Just then I came to the carefully sculptured avenue that leads down to the west, the sun behind me. And out of the trees nipped Doval, Zirk's out-circle Jang friend, afire with enthusiasm and importance.

"*Attlevey*," he drawled. "Got your svork?"

"Sword. Yes, I do."

"And your seconds?"

I looked at him sourly. Zirk really had been reading things up.

"No."

"Well, you ought to have seconds," said Doval. "Zirk has."

"Let me guess," I guessed. "You and Hergal."

"Kley and Hergal," Doval announced loftily.

"Female seconds aren't generally allowed," I said, "not if Zirk wants to follow the old customs accurately. Or has Kley changed?"

"No," said Doval. "She's just slavering to see you gutted."

"How sweet of her," I said.

We walked down the avenue together, Doval eyeing my fine-honed sliver-of-steel sword with contempt inadequately masking his interest. The house robots, which can be quite versatile with a bit of re-programming here and there, had

made the sword yesterday. They had been making my clothes
and other gear for two *vreks*.

"Danor not with you?" inquired Doval.

"Something wrong with your eyes, Doval?"

Danor had been tense and pale, so last night I'd slipped a
minor soporific in her snow-in-gold, and left her sleeping.
The swan was firmly anchored to the bed, its beak stuffed
three inches deep in a plate of swan-food.

The noise of the crowd was impressive now, and as we
emerged from the trees into the clearing Zirk had elected
for our duel, most of my fears were realized.

The bulk of the onlookers were Jang. Glittering and giggling, shoving, pushing, and gulping their pills, an enchanting picture they made. The air was full of their bees, bring-
ing them mirrors and scent and cigars and wine and meals
and pets. And every so often the bees would ram each other,
and Joyousness and bright-blue kicking animals would rain
upon the press below. Zirk, Hergal, Doval, and Kley between them had recruited their own bees to erect a temporary fence to hold the crowd back from the clearing. Some
terraces went up on the north and east sides, so they would
all get quite a decent view, damn them.

Zirk himself was sitting on a big platinum chair, stripped
to the waist. Somewhere in his reading he had been led
astray, for he was wearing a rather peculiar helmet, brazen
greaves and so on. Need I say he looked magnificent? Because he did, and also a complete idiot. Kley, in spiky
gold with gilt dragon heads pasted over her nipples, was
honing Zirk's sword personally, and sparks were flying.
Hergal lounged in the shade, handsomely bored. I could see
he was regretting the inconvenience already—was I worth
all this trouble? The rest of the circle were there too. Thinta
in pale-green see-through with a cat or two hooked on;
Mirri, a male for once, being very obviously married to
Thinta and making sure I noticed it. I even detected Hatta
by a blunder of scarlet among the glass shrubbery.

Doval strutted up to Zirk and said something. Zirk
grinned, Hergal yawned. The circle clustered together and
looked at me out of their cozy togetherness. Then Mirri de-
tached himself and came over.

"I've said I'll be your second, since you haven't got one, you
thalldrap."

Hatta, tripoddling up behind on his three legs, said:

"Me, too. You may need us."

"May I?"

"Zirk will rip you in shreds," said Mirri, twisting his mustache playfully. "So you're going to have a painful time till you get to Limbo."

Everyone seemed so certain Zirk was going to finish me that I suppose I might have relaxed with a happy sigh and just let events take their course. However, I've never been a lover of pain—I'm a whimpering coward, in fact—and I could just see me, bleeding slowly and agonizingly away in the silk-grass while Kley or somebody misled the robot rescue planes just long enough to make sure I got the most of it. Naturally, you couldn't really fool them, and they'd save me in the end; they always do. But for someone who flies to the medicinal-salve-dispenser for a hangnail, the prospect was unpleasing.

"Aren't you pale?" said Mirri. "Scared?"

"Shut up," said Hatta. "If you're his second, you're supposed to be on his side."

I won't say Hatta's loyalty touched me, but his stolid sense of fairness certainly brought a note of humor to the *drumdik* scene.

The Jang crowd, meanwhile, were setting up a hooting howl for us to begin. Zirk stood up and cracked his muscles loudly. Doval, primed in the formalities, came over and offered me wine, which I refused. Zirk swilled his mouth and spat, all brutal, on the quartz flowers. Then he marched into the clearing's center and Kley brought him the sword. It was a sort of cleaver, notched here and there to suggest previous (nonexistent) fights. Zirk had certainly caught the spirit of the thing.

I, modest sword in hand, joined him.

"Right," said Zirk. "To the death. Agreed?"

He really was about twice the size of me, and, for a couple of splits, I wished I'd done as he suggested, and got Limbo to fit me up with a new heroic body. His sword was definitely nasty, and bloodlust gleamed in his eye. And there stood my lovable circle, hoping for, and anticipating, my demise. My vitals turned over and icy sweat threatened my brow. But I nodded and smiled in true histrionic fashion.

"Ready when you are, *floop*."

And sword clanged on sword, as they say. Sword also clanged on air and tree bole—Zirk's sword, that is. I'd temporarily forgotten how much more agile slight, poetic me

DRINKING SAPPHIRE WINE 35

was than this musclebound freak. Besides, I had the art of it
somewhat, while he obviously believed he only had to swing
at me heartily and presently he'd cleave me from crown to
crotch. Which, left to himself, he probably would have done
eventually. But he wasn't left to himself, not quite. Two
things had happened. Some of the skill I'd learned over my
vreks of practice-fencing asserted itself automatically. I
found myself parrying and riposting very adequately in all
directions on a pure reflex. Additionally, my peerless cowardice had turned into a bright-red anger, which mounted and
blazed the longer I fought him. It wasn't like any of those
noble fighting dreams I'd ever programmed for myself. I was
just shaking and snarling with fury at the meanmindedness of
them, the way they'd ejected their stupid little poison-sacs
at me. Maybe, too, there was something of the old rage on
me, the rage against our whole way of living, our mores and
our superficial codes.

It was quite warm by now, and I could just hear the
squealing and yelping of the Jang crowd beyond the barrier
—experiencing our battle secondhand, as we all did most
events—but everything seemed to be coming from miles off.

Just then the edge of Zirk's cleaver slashed diagonally
over my chest. It bit through velvet and satin-of-steel shirt,
and through me.

There was no pain for a moment, as if my body didn't
realize what had happened to it. Then the pain did come, a
white zinging pain from shoulder to ribs. It felt as if he had
laid bare tissue and bone, but there was no chance to look,
luckily. Blood, my blood, was running exuberantly from
the wound, as if it had been waiting for ages only for a
chance to get free of the skin envelope, and now, burbling
to itself, fled like the kids at hypno-school at midperiod.

I knew enough to guess that the more I bled, the less
chance I had of getting Zirk. Which was splendid, wasn't it?
Just what I wanted?

Then I saw Zirk's face.

It had tightened, knotted up. It had a look of alarm, even
of fright. He was a mirror. I saw what I had become by looking at him. And I understood then that I was going to kill
him. Strive as I might, I couldn't stop myself.

I don't know how long it took. Not long, I suppose. From
the moment I admitted my desires, I seemed to open up
and catch fire. I didn't feel any danger from him. I found
after that he'd nicked me again once or twice, but nothing

like the first time. At this stage I was driving him back, the way you drive a reluctant house machine back into the wall, back and back.

Suddenly he collided with a tree. His arms went wide, he aimed a mad blow at me and missed me, and I went in under his arm, catching him hard in the thigh. He screamed in agony, a deep bellowing scream, connected with his bulk. It was like a cry out of prehistory indeed. It seemed to silence the whole city, let alone the crowd in Ilex Park.

I could have left him like that, to pump out his life there, as I thought he'd have left me. But instinct, which had possessed me, was too thorough, too clean. As he was falling, eyes rolling, mouth stretched over his teeth, I struck at his heart. He made no other sound, merely crashed like a colossus in the silk-grass, his weight tearing the sword from my hand. I could never have come near his heart unless he'd been on the way down; he was too tall.

6

They flew at me in unison, and at once.

"What a fight!" said Mirri, squeezing my arm, and I could see his male eyes already looking forward to the next female session he planned with me. *"What a fight!"*

Thinta and her cats meowed in my ears, which were beginning to din thickly:

"Ooma, are you all right?"

"He's excellent," said Kley. "That hulking dope didn't stand a chance."

Even Doval was smirking: *"Ever* so good."

Only Hergal wasn't there—looking green, he'd gone behind a tree. I could conjecture how he felt. There was no triumph now, only a grizzly, clammy horror, heightened by the extraordinary attitude of my friends, not to mention the crowd, most of whom were dissolving into hysterics of nausea or delight. The blood loss was telling also, and any split I was going to repeat my famous action of twelve *vreks* ago, and faint dead at their spangled feet.

Above, dimly heard by me, the wailing of robot sirens as the rescue squad homed in on Zirk. The sirens seemed to fill my lungs and push them out of my temples. Then a solid bulk inserted itself between me and the black pit I was about to fall backward into. Some kind of strong hand got hold of me, and I became aware, through the swarming black stars that were invading my eyes, of a scarlet presence on my left.

"Hang on to me," said Hatta in a voice so full of conspiracy that a feeble laugh reverberated my shattered frame. "Or do you fancy being carted to Limbo too, along with Zirk's last body?"

"No thanks. Hatta, you're amazing."

Hatta got me around, and we began to make it toward the avenue and away from the clearing. Not even Thinta, apparently, tried to stop us; maybe they were fascinated with the approaching Limbo team—I was too far gone to see or care.

37

Hatta, three-legged monster that he was, managed me reasonably well, but somewhere on the avenue I imagine I dropped in my tracks, for the next thing I knew I was hanging over his unrestful balloon shoulder, and we were jogging along at a cracking pace.

"Hatta," I mumbled, "do you have to run so fast? Two legs would be bad enough."

"Clearly," said Hatta, "you don't know what you've done, do you?"

"I think so."

"Then if you know, you'll know why I'm going fast."

My head swam with the motion of our career. I could no longer feel the wound of Zirk's sword. I must have said so, for Hatta panted:

"I put stuff on it, of course. Now quiet."

Quiet came, black as the mountains of the desert, soft as Danor's hair.

7

I woke to find the swan seated on my belly, dulcetly singing: "You are the wonderful sun of my sky." I took this initially as a sentimental gesture of concern for me on the swan's part, and was quite moved, until I recollected that this particular ditty seemed to be its method of calling for help. I struggled up and discovered, sure enough, that it had got its leash—snapped again—tangled around the bed legs, and was slowly strangling. I released it with some difficulty, and it strode out in search of Danor or food, or both.

The windows had been clouded. I cleaned them. Outside it was night, the sky glowing with stars and flash signs.

I felt almost normal, and the sword slash had healed completely in response to Hatta's quick-cure salve. It could only have been a flesh wound after all, though a bad one.

Hatta had apparently brought me home, also. A noble gesture, or maybe he was just nosy and/or after Danor.

There was no sign of either of them, but, following a split or two during which I warded off urgent robot plates with viands and noticed that the recluse switch was firmly depressed, I picked up the sound of their voices in the garden.

For some reason, or perhaps it was obvious, I guessed they were talking about me, so I sneaked toward the door and leaned there.

It was a strange sight, an azure angel in conversation with a red balloon, and, midway between them, the swan staring up at the dome-sky in a bemused yet creative fashion, as if trying to fathom the secrets of the universe.

"It's all so silly," Danor was saying vehemently. "So stupid, so silly, like everything else."

"It may be," said Hatta, "but the fact remains that it's a Committee order."

"It must have happened before," said Danor, "sometime."

"Never, they say. At least, not on city record. The notion of crime has been abolished for *rorls*, so they don't know

39

what to do. That means they'll invent things, and that means a superlative screwup."

Stunned by Hatta's perception, rancor, and colourful choice of words, I emerged on the marble terrace, and Danor jumped guiltily.

"What Committee order?" I inquired.

But they burst out, Danor:

"How could you leave me behind like that?"

And Hatta:

"How long have you been there?"

I said:

"You were involved enough, Danor. About one split, Hatta. I repeat—what Committee order?"

"A Committee messenger bee came while you were sleeping," said Danor. "They want you and each of us at the Committee Hall in Second Sector tomorrow, first thing."

"Surprise, surprise," I said. It sounded but too familiar. "And how's Zirk?"

"They've kept him in Limbo for observation," said Danor.

"Nice for them."

"You ought to take this seriously," said Hatta.

"How will that help?"

We sat and stared at the pool.

The swan teetered to the edge, but Hatta flapped it away again with his bizarre arms.

"You, er, you know I'll stick by you," said Hatta.

"Please," I said, "I've got enough problems without that."

"Oh, *ooma*—" said Danor.

"Oh *ooma* nothing. If he 'sticks by me' at the Hall looking like that, they'll slap a I.A. First-Class Maladjusted label on him from the start, and what good will that be to me, might I ask?"

"You are a bastard," said Hatta, unnerving me again slightly, for strong language, even when obsolete, was not generally his province.

"No such thing, Hatta, not any more. Been in the History Tower too?"

"I've been just about everywhere you've been, and you know why," said Hatta.

Yes, I knew why. Hatta loved me, and once, when I had been broken in pieces by everything and he arrived on my porch with hair the color of honey and a body fair as morning . . . I'd only got to dig up my metal-tape saga from twelve *vreks* ago to find that dismal story.

"Get going, Hatta," I said. And Hatta, as ever, got.

"You're very unkind to him," said Danor.

"I suppose Kam would have acted differently?"

She looked at me.

"Yes, Kam would."

"But Kam wasn't Jang," I said. "Jang—Jang—bloody Jang."

We sat silently in the garden for some while, and the swan careered about in the flowers, occasionally falling down or singing: "The wild white magic of your hair, the warm mauve magic of your eyes, both drive me *zaradann*."

I wondered if I'd see my old Q-R of the water carpet, the poor sod who'd formerly nursed me through my successive ambitions—the anti-Jang change, the work search, and my last scheme to make a child, which ended in such horror and wretchedness. However, there was neither sight nor sign of him. Maybe he'd had to be dismantled after his dealings with me—the strain must have been considerable. Or possibly he was just keeping out of my way—ditto.

Danor came with me, which I could have done without. I anticipated a grim sequence ahead.

We went through the usual Committee Hall routine of tunnel-rides, flying floors, waiting areas, and finally emerged in a circular cold-cream room with seats in tiers, mostly empty, and a central dais, mostly full. Q-Rs with miserably stern faces were packed onto it, their memory units and what-have-you no doubt clacking and clonking away in their joints. The people back on the tiers were all Older, and obviously had some vague status—doubtless merely titular—in the running of the city Committee affairs. Along the edges of the dais, like a garish flower bed, sat just about every Jang I had a nodding acquaintance with in Four BEE. Not to mention my circle. Kley, female; Mirri, female—fast work, she must have overdosed her meal injections again; Thinta, female of course, but no cats—probably forcibly torn from her at the entrance; even Hergal, male, and neurotic at being here and covering by slumping in attitudes of defiant nonchalance; and, at the very end, a tiny, delicate, perky little creature, tinkling crystals, with pale-pink satin lotus buds in her hair the exact exquisite tint of her mammalian tips, *Zirk!*

I burst into raucous laughter at that, overwrought as I was, and had to be restrained. Danor tugged at my arm, bees zoomed, Q-Rs flapped, and Older People muttered disparagingly. A male Jang appeared at my side.

"Get a grip on yourself," he said.

"Get a grip on your *graks*," I suggested. He was nothing special, gray and gross, an unimaginative haphazard body choice, but at least no duplicate limbs or heads, and no scarlet: it was Hatta come back to be my Tower of Strength.

"It's Hatta," said Danor.

"I know. Who else could it be? How'd you change so fast, Hatta? Your thirty units weren't up."

"Never mind that," said Hatta, embarrassed by his selfless act—he detested suiciding. "I took your point last night."

We had reached the dais, and were now separated. I found myself right in the middle of everything—room, Q-Rs, Jang, the lot. An unenviable position.

I tried to relax, but it was difficult. Muscles tensed and the skin twitched under my shadowy poet's eyes.

Everyone was fluttering and whispering. Nobody actually came out with a direct sentence. I looked around at them and beamed beneficently. "Well, isn't this fun?" I said in a loud voice.

It brought the Q-Rs to attention, as I'd suspected it might. One in the center, an important-looking being in gold, rapped on the little table in front of him.

"You will kindly not display levity. This is a very dreadful situation," he said.

"Oh, *awful*," I agreed. "Poor Zirk cut down in his prime, and back five splits later looking like a refrigerated silk flower."

Zirk jumped up and began to squeak malevolently at me, with crystalline tears welling from her dusky eyes. Other Jang joined in, and the gold Q-R rapped and rapped until a gong went off somewhere, and everybody stopped shouting in surprise.

"This inquiry will be conducted with propriety," thundered the Q-R, rather optimistically. He turned to me. "You will now give us an account of what precisely led up to this unfortunate event, whose significance, clearly, few of you comprehend."

"All right," I said. "One day when I was standing outside Silver Mountain, Zirk—male, and about the size of a small museum—knocked me flying and challenged me to a duel. That is—"

"Yes," said the Q-R. "We have looked up dueling in the files and we know."

"I agreed to the duel, and we met in Ilex Park, where, due to superior skill and more practice, I won. Zirk is now happily installed in a new body, and everything, I should have thought, is *insumattly derisann*."

There were some laughs at this, which the Q-R ignored. "It is not," he said. "Neither is that a full account."

"Oh, well, I do apologize. I thought it was. Of course, I omitted to say that Ilex Park at the time was its usual uninspired jade-green and the dome sun was rising in its usual damn silly way and the dry ice was puffing about nicely all over us. Is that better?"

"You will be silent," said the Q-R.

"Don't bank on it."

"You will be silent," went on the Q-R, "or you will be silenced by hypno-spray. Which?"

"I'll be silent," I agreed.

"Jang Zirk," said the Q-R, "perhaps you'd give us your version."

Zirk got up again, balancing precariously on her weeny silver-slippered feet. She dabbed her eyes and said, huskily now: "I see it was ever so *selt*—er—foolish of me. But I, um, lost my temper." She tittered like a peal of bells. Just think of Zirk loosing her temper, ooh! How quaint of her.

"Permission to speak," I said. They looked at me. "If Zirk continues like this, I'm going to be ill all over your lovely white room."

I shouldn't have risked it, but I was past reason. Giggles filled the air, Zirk stamped and nearly fell down. Next second a cool rain dropped on me from an overhead bee, and I was rendered duly limp and speechless, only my ears and eyes and brain left ticking, which I could have foregone.

And Zirk *was* continuing.

"It was just the way he lied to us all and carried Danor off. I mean, we were all so *frightfully* anxious to meet her! And then, not marrying! So shocking to avoid a Jang custom like that. Well, I just got ever so angry"— eyelashes flittered, mouth pouted—"and when I *met* him, I just couldn't control myself. Oh dear. And we've been such sweethearts in the past, he and I. I couldn't *tell* you the times we've married and had love. Oh, there I go, digressing. Well, I only meant it to be a sort of friendly bout. But he went *zaradann—zaradann*, I tell you. I've *never seen* such a thing." Zirk clasped her pink-nailed hands and sighed with terror. "He cut me down without mercy."

8

After Zirk, everyone had a say.

Thinta said I'd always been unstable, but it was my temperament, and I meant well. She hoped the Committee realized that she'd been a good influence on me, and had always tried to keep me out of trouble.

Kley said I ought to be whipped, and volunteered to do it.

Mirri said Zirk had wounded me and I'd played quite fairly. She said I was mad but she didn't mind. She said Danor had forced me into acting ignorantly and thoughtlessly, and the Committee ought to ship her back to BAA.

Hergal said I'd killed Zirk deliberately (he was the first to use the word "kill"). He added that Zirk asked for it and would have got me if he'd been able. The Committee then asked Hergal about my earlier challenge to himself, and Hergal told them, in detail. He said I was predominantly female and needed a sex change back and that was all that was wrong with me and could he go now because he was fed up with being there. The Committee said no.

Danor looked as pale as I'd designed myself to be, and gorgeous. She said calmly that it had been a mutual decision for us to go away alone together and to have love without marrying. We hadn't meant to upset anybody. The Committee said hadn't she spent a lot of time with an Older Person in BAA without marrying, and hadn't the Committee there advised them to part? I could see her hands trembling when she answered yes, that was so, looking at them straight on and not lowering her voice. The Jang gasped and exclaimed at her daring and obscenity and were gonged into quiet. The Committee said that her actions were curious and showed unusually antisocial tendencies. Danor did not answer, but when she sat down again she shut her eyes as if she were very tired.

Hatta said my first challenge to Hergal had been a joke, and Zirk was a fool. He said Zirk had meant to kill me (other Jang later supported this, recalling Zirk's threats to me outside Silver Mountain). Hatta said I hadn't meant to kill Zirk, only incapacitate him, but Zirk fell on my sword. There was an outcry at this.

Doval said I was terrific with a sword and I'd known exactly what I was doing when I went for Zirk. Doval said he hoped the Committee would make dueling a regular pastime in the parks, and a roar of delight drowned even the gong.

Several out-circle Jang girls said I was wonderful, and several out-circle Jang males said I used to be all right when I was female. One male said if I ever came near his circle he'd meet me in Ilex Park and do better than Zirk did.

Altogether, everyone more or less said different things, and nobody really fully agreed with anyone else, either about me or what I had done.

About nine thousand mealtimes had gone by, and the Jang were noisily pleading for food. Even the pompous Older People looked uncomfortable.

At length the gold Q-R announced that if we went next door, we should discover sustenance, but we should come back in an hour when we heard the gong. To begin with I thought I would be left in my hypno-sprayed condition, alone and foodless, but a bee came over and shot me full of something, and I got to my feet all faculties restored.

I took Danor's hand as the crowd went milling ahead.

"I can't tell you how sorry I am," I said.

"Then don't tell me," she answered, softly, smiling, still Danor.

Gray Hatta came up.

"You should have done what they said," he predictably told me.

We went through into a merry yellow room where the Jang were falling on nut-steak, wine-cakes, and rock-cherries with shrill cries. The Older People had gone off somewhere more peaceful to stuff themselves.

"What would you like, Danor?" asked Hatta politely.

"Oh, nothing, thank you."

"Nor me," I said.

"You must eat," instructed Hatta.

Zirk came floating up then, a couple of males trailing her interestedly. Both bore a distinct resemblance to Zirk's male bodies, a strange phenomenon I had noted before here and there. Maybe everyone only wants to have love with themselves really.

"*Attlevey*," said Zirk to me, lowering her pastel lids. "I do so hope you didn't mean those *drumdik* things you said about me, *ooma*. When this nasty business is over, possibly we could meet and have a talk about everything, um, do you think?"

"Zirk," I said, "you may be steeped in scent and prisms, with a waist the width of my wrist, but if you don't beat it, I'm going to tip the nearest jug of silver-cordial right down your cleavage."

"Here now," boomed Zirk's escort in bass voices. They were waving their ten-ton fists aloft when Mirri thrust between them.

"*You!*" she yelled at Zirk, "you're worse than *her!*" indicating Danor. "I think you've got an absolutely *farathooming* nerve." And she slung a bowl of rock-cherries in Zirk's powdered face and began to pull out her curled flaxen hair in handfuls while Zirk screamed pitifully.

Zirk's two champions tried to rescue her, and someone who fancied Mirri came haring across to rescue *her*. Presently, chaos reigned.

Danor, Hatta, and I, for once in agreement, shrank to the side as an incredible Jang fight broke out in every direction. Some were siding with Mirri, some with Zirk. Some were just enjoying themselves. Nuts, cakes, and bubbling liquor flew through the air, and shrieks and crashes resounded.

Suddenly a siren tore across the uproar. An amplified Q-R voice bellowed: "Cease fighting at once or you will be sprayed."

Violence faltered and petered out. Jang stood staring about, their clothes in ribbons and their faces daubed with bruises and crushed-orange.

"You will return in orderly fashion to the Inquiry Hall. Take your seats, and remain silent."

It was just like hypno-school. Which, considering the recent antics, was not to be wondered at.

Everybody filed docilely through and sat, surreptitiously brushing off their see-throughs and getting cake out of their jewelry. The Q-Rs were still on the dais, but a look of abject horror had settled on their faces. They were well and truly scared—not for themselves, for their programming doesn't really allow them that, but for us, for what we might do to each other.

When everything was quiet enough to hear the dust-absorbers at work in the ceiling, the gold Q-R rose to his feet and focused on me.

"We have come to a decision," he said.

Up till that instant, despite my earlier—disregarded—caution, I hadn't credited the situation with too much importance. It was harrowing only because of its stuffiness. Cities run by robots and androids specifically geared to serve the community didn't intimidate anyone that much. I hadn't expected them to take any vital action, beyond another inconvenient black mark against me and some sort of piddling little reprimand, and perhaps a restriction, like putting the parks off limits to me for fifty units or something. Punishments were never used and fines were extinct. The only powers ever exercised were always, however exacerbating, supposed to be for your own good in the end.

But something in the Q-R's somber tone sent white-hot sparks through my innards.

"We want everyone to understand this," said the Q-R, glancing about at the Jang witnesses. "The notion of crime was abolished long since, so it has not been easy for us to determine what we should do. We have comprehended that the Jang Zirk was the aggressor in this particular instance, and that, had the circumstances been reversed, he would be sitting now where the Accused is sitting." A murmur at that "Accused." The Q-R continued: "Nevertheless, as under the ancient laws which preceded our present data, it is the actual Killer who is to pay the penalty."

No murmur at that second word. It struck too deep, like the very blade I'd used. Killer. I have killed, therefore I am a—

"Also, by reference to certain zoom-scan pictures recorded in the Flash Center, we have observed the face of the Accused during the combat. Unmistakably, the intent to kill was present." The Q-R turned again to me. "It is a rare occurrence. Or it was. Since death no longer exists, the desire to kill—founded as it was on the idea of being rid of something—has mainly atrophied. Where it has not, the Dream Rooms and Adventure Palaces have diverted the emotion along harmless channels. Now, however, one of you *has* killed—not himself, which is his right, but another against his will, and the fancy may well take root in many minds. Look at the violence already unleashed, look at yourselves. Although anyone murdered in the city can be reclaimed immediately at

Limbo as with a suicide, this does not detract from the frightfulness of the act of Murder itself, and it is on this premise that we have passed sentence. You had better remain sitting," he added to me, quite compassionately, so I guess I'd attempted some stab at getting up, but my legs had gone to jelly and I hadn't made it. "There is a choice," he said. "Please consider carefully. You will have three units in which to do so. Firstly, you may go to Limbo and experience Personality Dissolution. As you know, this means your consciousness will be darkened and your memory wiped clean. As is usual, you will re-emerge three *rorls* from now and resume life in the cities, unhampered by past guilt, or by these antisocial drives which have grown up in you (this last merely the culmination of many suspect misdemeanors, one of which, we remind you, concerned the destruction of your unborn baby due to sheer folly on your part). When you leave PD yours will be an entirely changed ego. You will commence again at the child stage, as is general, with a suitable Q-R guardian, knowing only that you are returning, but recalling nothing, either of this current era, or of your present personality. Normally PD is performed for those who have lived many *rorls* and feel the urge to slough the mental accumulations of time. In your case, it is considered a cardinal condition, if you are to remain as a citizen of the Fours."

No noise in the great circular room. I couldn't even hear my heart beating. If it was.

The Q-R narrowed his eyes as if what he told me hurt him.

"The alternative to loosing your identity and your individuality so soon is this: that you leave the dome four units from today, and exist thereafter in the desert, in exile, denied access to Four BEE, Four BAA, and Four BOO for the indefinite period of your natural human span—which might possible continue anything up to a *rorl*. You will be supplied, of course, with every life support and commodity you may ask for, within reason. Also you will be permitted, before your departure, one final body choice, so that you can design a body best suited to your needs and your situation. Additionally, your location will be monitored, and, should you require medical or other functional aid, it will be sent you. Otherwise no contact with any city or citizen will be granted you. The disadvantages of this alternative are several, as you can perceive. Loneliness and fear are hazards. And, as your body grows older, it will age, an unpleasant process, not recommended. In the end, provided you do not suicide before, a natural death will terminate your life, after which the city will reclaim you, and PD will be carried out in any case, in order that finally you may be returned into the social structure of Four BEE."

He folded his hands.

"In either circumstance, every one of your present relationships, intimate or otherwise, is over forever. On your re-emergence, three *rorls*—or more—from today, your contemporaries may have passed themselves voluntarily into Personality Dissolution, and even if they have not, you will never remember them nor they you in your reawakened form. Not one here with you at this moment will you be likely to call lover or friend again in the future."

Abruptly the heavy quiet was broken. Some Jang girl was wailing that they couldn't do it to me, it was ghastly, unspeakable. I think I'd only married her for a unit once, about a *vrek* before.

"This choice," our instructor cut in and silenced her, "is the only one you are offered. There is no other way. You must resign yourself, and decide. *Rorls* in the past, you yourself would have met death—actual and total death. Obliteration—as the punishment for your crime. We have tried to act in your ultimate best interests as well as those of the community at large, and it has cost us a great deal of energy and time. You have three units, no more, no less. Sort out your affairs and consider your plans carefully. As for the rest of the Jang in this room, we hope you will take the warning to heart. Please now, go home."

They hurried by me as though I had plague.
I had.
Thinta and Mirri were crying, even Kley was crying. Hergal looked as sick as he had in the park. Zirk too. No doubt she was thinking that but for my fencer's skill, this choice would have been hers to make, not mine.

The Q-Rs also stole away, and the Older People. Eventually I was left with only Hatta and Danor.

I wondered dully if Hatta would say "I told you so." He didn't. He stood staring into nothing. I'd forgotten he loved me, or thought he did. It was in some ways almost as shattering a blow for him, for he was going to lose me forever and a unit.

Danor put her face against mine. There were no tears on her cheek, yet the sorrow hung on her like a sad smoky perfume.

"Danor," I said, "hold me. Don't let me go."

9

You bet I had a party. It was the inevitable thing to do. The extreme reaction which extremity forces you into.

Besides, everyone predicted I'd give a party. They also predicted that at the height of the festivity and abandon, I'd leap from a roof or dive into a pool without an oxygen injection and not swimming, or maybe, if their luck was really in, douse myself with Joyousness and strike an igniter in my ear. That was the only way to behave, after all. For there was only one answer to my choice of alternatives—die and let Limbo destroy my soul, or at any rate, wash it spotless and characterless. Three *rorls* of oblivion, followed by a repeat childhood and permanent amnesia, were a dire fate for a Jang, a crushing blow none of them spoke of, but which you could tell they were considering from the way the color fled their cheeks. But the other thing, exile and despair among the dunes, companionless till the end of my days, growing dry as the sand, creaky and wizened as the cacti, and agoraphobia everywhere—never, never! If, by some master stroke of insanity, I had accepted that, I would put paid to myself inside a quarter *vrek* anyway. So, glorious, tumultuous suicide *now* it would have to be. Go out with a bang, *show* everyone what I was made of . . .

They were so interested in what I'd do, so fascinated by the notion of my macabre farewell feast, they forgot or mislaid their revulsion at my contaminating doom, and flocked around me from sunrise to sunrise.

I wondered if one or both of my makers—last seen many moons ago—might signal me, to say goodbye, or something. Anything. But they didn't. Probably they were both in Boo or Baa, and didn't get to hear of it or even realize it was me, their child, until it was too late.

Under sentence, I felt hollow, pithless. The first and second units of the time they'd allowed me, I woke with a feeling of blind clawing terror. The second unit I wept, and Danor wept with me.

She asked me if she should go, but I said stay. I needed her, or thought I needed her, I don't know why, because it didn't really help, though she was steady and tender. The swan wandered about peeing on things and falling on things. The swan saved us a little, but only a little. I made an arrangement for Danor to have my home after I was . . . no longer in residence.

One excellent fact: everything I bought was free, including the extra novelties for the party. I suppose the Committee understood I was incapable, in the circumstances, of groveling out thank-yous in a pay booth.

Nearly all Four BEE's Jang must have come to that party, or it seemed like it.

It was my last night in the world, and I'd taken enough ecstasy to launch a small rocket into space. I was absolutely numb with it, couldn't feel a thing; even the prospect before me seemed unimportant, bearable almost. So what were three *rorls*? There'd be other Danors. Hypno-school was OK, mainly you didn't know about it anyhow, and I was going to make an utter *promok* out of my Q-R guardian. My ego would strike back through the brainwashing and consciousness-darkening, somehow it would. I was incorrigible, wasn't I? So drink up and swallow the pretty pills, and goodbye Danor, how I'll miss your beautiful—better forget about that, my friend, if you're going to be a kiddy all over again in three *rorls*' time.

The whole riot took place in the Moon Gardens in Second Sector. Blue and green fireballs of non-hot flame lit the groves of filigree trees. The fountains ran with blue wine, and a dragon or two from BAA glittered here and there, and BAA android females sang in sweet voices, plants growing from their heads and bursting into blossom. The sky was full of Jang riding starry birds, and rainbows, and golden-scented rain.

We also sang at the long tables, most of the vomitous Jang hit songs, delivering them with passion and sincerity. I was toying with the idea of slashing my wrists in an antique style of suiciding princes at feasts, but concluded I was too hazy with ecstasy to get it right, and abandoned the fancy. Then came the Masque of Death—a small entertainment I'd dreamed up that evening to give them all colic.

I designed it via a thought-receptive screen, the sort of effort the Dream Rooms and the Picture-Vision places use. The resulting montage was thrown three-dimensionally out into the Moon Gardens, and grim and grand it was.

Six pairs of dancers, three male and three female, in emerald and scarlet velvet with golden-tassel hair. They danced and they embraced, they offered each other gifts and smiled into each other's eyes. Then came death—the Ego-Death of Limbo's PD. It was a black-enameled worm and its head was a white skull. It thrust between them and they were smitten in its coils. They lay on the grass like broken flowers and the worm laughed, and sang a brief song of my composing, telling how Ego-Death was best for them and the community. I must already have been fairly ecstatic when I invented that song. It was silly, garbled, and amazingly bitter and terrible, and you could see the Jang blanching at a distance of fifty paces. Then bells rang and the fallen dancers rose. They bowed to the worm, and went on bowing until they shrank down to the size of children. They didn't know who they were or who the others were, their friends and lovers, but ran off after the worm, kissing its oily tail, with blindfolds obscuring their eyes.

"That's it," Hergal said to me. He and Mirri were consoling each other. "That's absolutely it, old *ooma*. Blindfolds and *thalldrapping* worms."

Thinta lay in a fountain of Joyousness, meowing, and Kley had come as a male, pathetic and inhibited, his eyes red. Hatta kept pouring me wine, wine the color of sapphires. "Drink up," he said whenever I flagged. "Take another pill."

If Zirk was there, I never saw him, or her.

Suddenly it was very late, about two hours before dawn, and I'd disappointed the Jang by not suiciding, which dismally cheered me.

"Danor," I said, "let's go back home. For the last time."

So we went. Up Periot Waterway in an open boat, up the bright staircase, under the anemone opening and shutting on the porch. For the last time.

I was so drink-and-drug-sodden I didn't know if I could actually do anything, but some of Four BEE's pills are wonderful things, and paleness had touched the sky when we lay stilled and silent in each other's arms. And I recalled that night so long ago when impotence had ravaged us, and it had *mattered* and meant so *much*.

Danor said quietly:

"I loved this time we've had. After Kam, it's meant a lot to me. I'm only sorry, so sorry—"

"Don't talk about it," I said. "It's nearly here."

And then I fell asleep, abruptly, as if I could escape that way from what came closer with every split.

I was standing by the pet's grave. My pet from all the *vreks* before. My pet who died on the shock wall the day after the great rains, when the desert blossomed. City robots from Limbo had buried it, at my request, out in the sands beyond the dome, because I couldn't let them incinerate its white body, like a fall of snow, in some neat, hygienic pet cremator. I'd never known the site of the grave; I hadn't gone with them. Yet here I was.

All around was desert and the dust wind softly blowing, but I scarcely noticed it yet. For on the grave sat the pet itself, washing with an infuriatingly thorough concentration. Then it looked up at me, a couple of its six white legs still hooked at amazing angles around its head, looked out of its orange eyes.

"You're dead," I said to the pet. "True death. Obliteration."

"Certainly my body's dead," said the pet casually, "but whoever told you that everything else dies with it? What about that thing they use at Limbo, the thing the androids don't have, the life spark, the soul? My, my, have *you* been led by the nose."

Of course, the pet had never been able to talk—one of its virtues, maybe. It didn't even seem to be talking now, yet somehow I heard the words, and imagined they came from it.

"Why am I here?" I asked.

"Why indeed? Obviously, you'd much rather stay in the city and get washed out, or whatever it is."

"Oh, you're wrong. I'm afraid to wake up, because then I have to go and let them do it."

"Why do you? They're only a bunch of dopey quasi-robots trying to work out all the answers, and getting tied up in their rewire circuits. As for you, have you forgotten *everything?*"

"How else could I get by, without making myself forget?" I said, and didn't at first know what I meant.

"Finally you can only get by by letting yourself remember. Look."

And we were up in a bird-plane, but it was open all around so you could see every way at once, and feel the scratchy wind and smell the sand and rock smell, and the smell of the wide sky.

Dark sky, even at noon, sky of an indigo greenness, sky with a blinding, scorching sun, a sun in space, not a mechanism revolving in a dome roof like a child's toy. Below, the land, the pale dunes, the black mountains shaped like spears, like towers, like fortresses. On the horizon one volcano pouring its crimson plume into the air, fierce, uncompromising, and real. A wild land, a cruel land, a land to catch you out, bury you in sandstorm, broil you under the sun, freeze you under the stars, dehydrate and suffocate you in the heat with its low oxygen count. A land to thrill and humble you in that single unit after the rains, when all the barren sand is bright with green, and ferns spring toward the mountains and cover their flanks like a rolling ancient sea.

"Here I am!" shouted the desert, loud with life, for life there still was in it, waiting, stored, like seed. "Here I am. Did you forget me? Forget me despite your dreams of me, your dreams of the sun and the rain and the antique tribes who roamed me once with their herds and their weird ways? You, who moaned and whined, covering metal-tape with cries and yearning, you, you effete *thalldrap?* Now's your chance to prove you can do more than sit on your tail complaining and drinking sapphire wine with your tears of self-pity. Come on, come and do battle with me, come and fight me. I'm more than a match for you. I'll devour you if I can, but I'll do it cleanly and openly, not with words and dark little tanks in Limbo. Don't be afraid of human death and human age. I've seen it all, and I know it. It's just dust blown over the rocks. Look at me, how dead and old I seem, and yet, watch me grow, watch me live. Come on. Come and find me. I'm waiting."

"Pet," I said, "I've forgotten your name."

"Names," said the pet. "Is that the only thing you care about?"

And it bit me hard, so hard I woke up with a shout.

10

I went into the foyer of the Committee Hall in Second Sector, and quite a big silent crowd was standing there, gawping. There were messenger bees too, and zoom-scanners zooming in from the nearest Flash Center, since I and my fate were exciting news, the first bit of drama for sixty *rorls* or whatever it was.

"Please follow me," said a tactful Q-R. "I'm sure you'd prefer to do this in private."

"No, thanks," I said. "I'll give my decision publicly, out here. After all, everybody's so enthralled."

It was a grandiose and gloomy occasion. The Q-R slowly went away, and presently the others from the Inquiry came shoveling out, led by the spokesman in gold.

I won't say I wasn't shaking all over, and I won't, in fact, say any more about the state of my mind and my nerves, because they were fairly serious. But somewhere in me was a rod of steel to which I clung. I'd had a vision, as good as any vision given to any poet, sage, or prophet in the past. I wasn't elated, I wasn't confident even, but somehow, I *knew*, and with the end of doubt had come the death of despair.

"Fine," I said, when I saw their depressed, executioners' faces. "I hope everybody can hear me, and I hope the Flash Center is getting it too, because what I want to say is important, and it's just about time someone did say it. I'm only embarrassed it took this pseudo-trial to push me into making a move."

The Q-Rs began to look bothered. Was I going to create yet another disturbance? I went on fast, before they could start ordering sprays. "My decision is this: I'm heading into the desert."

There was an interruption at this point. The crowd set up a lot of noise, even the Q-Rs seemed to be buzzing, in the region of their necks. Then everyone was saying shut up, shut up, to each other, since they could see I hadn't finished. So I bowed, and continued:

57

"You think I've gone mad, and that's probably a logical assumption on your part. I'm scared, I'll admit, at what I'm going to do. But I tell you, we live here like a lot of embryos in a breeding tank. Every need is catered for. The Committee wipes our noses for us and picks us up when we fall down. Outside the domes we have a planet which actually belongs to us, and which half of us have never seen and would rather not see. I have seen it, and I like what I saw better than the sort of style and judgment you can see in Four BEE." I looked at the Q-Rs. "So I've got the list of my requirements drawn up, and, brace yourselves, it's a long one. And I'm ready, when you Q-R gentlemen are ready, to get down to it."

The gold Q-R said extremely clearly, as if explaining to an imbecile: "We hope you have not been hasty. This is serious."

"Don't I know it. I told you, I've made my choice. If you think you have some damn right to give me an alternative like the alternative you gave me, I think I have a right to pick which course I accept. I'll take the desert, and you can take Limbo PD and shove it right up your electronic valves."

I felt I was unfair to those Q-Rs, who were blindly serving the community, or attempting to, as their programming ensured they must. But then, how could anyone ask me to be otherwise? Nobody expects the condemned to embrace the axe.

But nobody expected either, at least I don't think they did (certainly I didn't), the cheer that went belting up from the crowd in the Hall. Even the people cheering seemed unnerved. They were cheering me. Not so much for my speech but for that very thing which so appalled them normally. Because I had defied the System, bitten again at the burning sun.

The cheers faded. A self-conscious void followed. Into the void, I spoke.

"Come on, then. Here's my list, a whole boxload of it. Let's not *grak* about."

Part Two

I got a sand-ship off them, and it wasn't easy.

If they exiled you to the desert, they reckoned they'd put up for you a nice little palace with every mod. con., and there you'd sit, *vrek* by *vrek*, staring up at the glassy ceiling, or down the vacuum drift or something, till boredom got the better of you, you selected a tasteful high window, and jumped out of it. I won't say they definitely encouraged you to suicide and get everything over with quickly (and so back into PD in civilized fashion), but the idea that survival might be wrested from the situation, purpose even, was clearly indigestible to them.

What did I want a sand-ship *for?* To be mobile, to move about in? Well, yes. But—I reasoned—it would save them a bird-plane trip for me going from the dome, and it would also save them time, energy, and building materials. A sand-ship came ready-fitted, of necessity, with all life-support systems—oxygen pump, provision dispenser, water mixer, freezer storage, heat and cooler units, stabilizers (essential since about two-thirds of the desert is earthquake zone), defense mechanisms, even service and maintenance robots. And there must be surplus ships. How often did they run? And even when they did, they mostly ran passengerless, citizens who traveled preferring planes and sky-boats, which, they felt, kept them at a safer distance from the agoraphobic waste. Think, I kept saying, of the bother it would save the Committee if they just gave me a sand-ship. And, at last, they reluctantly responded.

Of course, I was acting on impulse merely. I'd been in a sand-ship before, twice, and seen what they had to offer, but their mobility did head *my* list of favorables. I had some mad notion of fizzing along the desert by day and night, the Outcast, a dangerous hazard to authorized traffic, shouting embittered songs at the sun and stars. My future seemed bleak, so I had clothed it in colorful hysteria; that way it was almost tolerable.

By the end of the fourth unit, I had to be out of the city. I hadn't seen any "friends" since the party, nor Danor since our parting at dawn, when I had waked from the dream and wildly chittered my intentions in her ears. I was terrified she'd start trying to dissuade me—maybe succeed—but she only nodded. "Yes," she said. "I think you're right. Yes, yes. Go and tell them, *ooma*." The last embrace was hurtful, and better undescribed. I wanted no one to see me off. So, from the moment I left home, I was entirely isolated, already exiled, though, what with the cheering crowd, and the Committee Hall and Limbo swirling with Q-Rs, I scarcely felt it. Then came the last journey across Four BEE to the dome lock.

I was female again by then, which, hormone-wise, no doubt made everything much worse. But I'd had to opt for a sex change—Hergal probably vibrated with glee when he heard. This was the final body I'd ever be allowed until my "natural death," all of a *rorl* perhaps away. I was predominantly female, and I didn't dare risk that fact catching up with me out alone in the wild when I could no longer alter things. Besides, I'd had a generous portion of masculinity, and should have sated that side for some while. I didn't feel comfortable, though, being a girl again when really, under ordinary circumstances, I wasn't ready to be. I kept forgetting my physiognomy was different, which was embarrassing enough, and, seeing myself in mirrors, was startled and demoralized, despite the beauty I'd ordered in Limbo as my right.

And I was very beautiful. It was the most beautiful body I'd ever designed. I was going to have to live with it, literally, and watch it, too, decaying. It was, therefore, the sort of loveliness which is not perfect, but draws its charm from a measure of imbalance, which can accommodate flaws and make little of them, for a while at least. A slim, agile body for traversing harsh regions, excellent muscle tone, long legs, long fingers, breasts not too large—able to resist the sag that would come with *vreks* of gravity. Good bone structure in a face light and versatile, to hold that smooth flesh taut to the bitter (how bitter?) end. Oh, yes, I'd thought of everything, hadn't I? For, reading in the History Tower, I had learned fully of the myth of Old Age and the roads whereby it traveled.

My skin was tawny-tan to complement and survive the lashes of the sun, my hair one shade fairer than my skin, straight and bright as a tan flame. The poet's eyes I kept, the large blue opals with their shadowy rims. At least I could recognize their glances in the ambushing mirrors of the city I was leaving forever.

The bird-plane was anonymous. Two Q-Rs rode with me, innocuous guards.

I had never felt much for Four BEE beyond a kind of contemptuous familiarity. Now it didn't look dear to me, or precious, yet so known and so secure. Never again will I ride on Peridot Waterway, never again watch the tragic dragon spray its green fire before Jade Tower, never again wander the movi-rails beneath the artificial stars, or drink snow-in-gold at Blue Sky, or lie with some lover in the plastic-cloud floaters, or . . .

The poet's eyes were weeping down my girl-stranger's face, and with my unknown tawny slender hands I made obscure crushing gestures, as if it were my emotion I tried to crush.

At the lock, somehow, there was no crowd. Obviously secrecy and intrigue had been perpetrated to mislead the populace.

The sand-ship stood waiting there. I stared at it with icy fear, as if it threatened me, this thing which was to be my home.

Every scrap of my belligerence and my defiance had gone. The dream was insubstantial as smoke. I wanted to beg them to let me stay, but I knew they never would, so somehow kept my mouth shut.

They escorted me into the ship, my two Q-Rs. The robots were already busy here and there; the automatic motors were humming to be off. I didn't have to drive or navigate myself, of course. It would do everything itself, to my specifications. It wasn't a big ship, but pretty big for me. The Q-Rs showed me the monitor beam they'd put in, the thing I could use to signal the city for extra supplies or medical help. It would relay through a computer, naturally, and be very efficient, and that meant that, even in this way, I couldn't communicate with another human being. While I was myself, I would never hear a real human voice again. And, though I might see the bird-planes pass over, or distant sister ships go gliding by along the horizon of the dunes, never again would I see a real human face.

"All right," I said to the Q-Rs. "I understand where everything is." I hadn't had to pay for anything; I wouldn't ever have to pay from here on. One advantage of exile. I wiped the tears from my cheeks and glared my escort out. "Now, get off my ship."

They went immediately, and once the doors had shut, I flipped the switch for automatic drive.

The window-spaces were covered, but shortly there came the bang of the dome locks, closing behind me for the ultimate time.

I sat very still and very stiff upon the velvet seat, feeling the unseen desert clasp me round.

Alone at last.

2

How many times in the city I had longed for privacy, sought and won privacy, and sighed with relief. Privacy is a pleasant thing when crowds surge below and friends hammer, unheard, at the porch signal.

I got up eventually, and went about the ship. It thought for itself, and had no need of my supervision. Steady on its air cushions, it would swoop to port or starboard to avoid rocks or faults or exploding volcanoes. Clever ship. I could foretell I might begin to talk to it sooner or later, call it by a pet name; talk to the robots too, probably, program them to carry out inane tape-voice calls and motions of recognition when they saw me. No doubt I should murmur endearments to the love machine, pretend it was Danor, Lorun, Hergal . . . Oh, I could see everything before me, like pictures painted on my mind.

I chose a sleeping place, one of the several cabins the ship possessed. It was done up in cream and blue.

At least there'd be Picture-Vision, human bodies on perma-celluloid for me to watch. Song tracks to play and moving-picture magazines too, in the ship's store. And after all, ecstasy in abundance. If I planned it carefully, I could stay ecstatic for ten units at a time before I had to give it a rest. Because, even then, I knew I wasn't going to suicide. Oh no. However bad it got (and it was going to get bad, wasn't it?) I wouldn't give them the satisfaction.

I sat an hour or so in the pale-gold saloon under the chandelier, before a delicious untasted repast the robots had served. I'd already inspected the automatic food and water machines, marveling aloud, until I caught myself, on their intricate, self-maintaining activities.

The ship was still running, north, east, west, south— or in a circle—what did it matter? Solar battery by day, friction circuits by night, or during recharging. You could hear the systems change over, one to the other, if you listened hard.

I took a robot into one of the game rooms, and we played star-ball for a while, but I missed the bad language and the sulking or spiteful victory noises of a human opponent. Even when the ball went smack into the robot's faceplate, never a word. Just imagine Hergal—no, don't do that. Don't imagine anyone.

All this while, there had been one small part of me I had managed to keep hidden. The part which was thinking of the desert everywhere around. On my first sand-ship journey, I had run to the Transparency Tower in the stern to observe the landscape, and gone into euphorics over it. Now I wouldn't go there. I was afraid. Afraid to see and afraid to confront my reaction to seeing. As soon as I understood this, the evasion began to prey on me.

Nibble, nibble. Cowardice becomes you, *ooma*.

Go on, go on, get up and look.

'Fraid to face the nasty-wasty waste.

Nag, nag, nag.

At length I rose, girded my loins, so to speak, and skulked down the corridor.

On the sand-ship runs, the glacia-view of the towers clouds and clears in spasms, to lessen the shock. Most passengers go crazy and foam at the mouth when they see the desert: I never had, and my hauteur had known no bounds. But this time I'd been hoping, I think, that the glacia-view would be opaque. However, it was night outside, and the towers stay clear nocturnally, presumably judging everyone a-bed.

Desert night. Yes, I'd forgotten.

Pale sand hills, seas of sand under the stars, black crags supporting black sky. To the west, one of the ubiquitous eruptions going on, but so distant as to be only an enlarged sequin on the dark. And yes, it was powerful, beautiful, but it was unfriendly, cruel, vast, limitless. And I was afraid. It wasn't like the dream.

Nowhere to run now, but to this inhospitable land.

Go to the sand and say: Help me. Go to the rock and ask it for love and kindness.

The stars stare down, the bones of the planet stare up, and I am caught between as if on the points of two daggers.

The tower, clear on every side and above, seemed swimming around me in a blur of black and paleness. I clutched at objects in panic, as if to prevent myself from falling from a great height, and accidentally activated a siren which went whooping off in the ceiling. This saved me, by a hair's breadth, from something I had no name for, pure insanity, maybe. I bashed at buttons, and the siren relapsed into silence. Then, I fled from the tower and into my safe cabin with its window-spaces of solid blue brocade.

I lay among the gauzes of the anchored float-bed, crying soundlessly. For, having come to fight the desert, I couldn't even face it now, I, who had danced, so long ago with my pet, among its rain-green dunes.

Three units and three nights we ran, the ship and I. I lay on my bed and the machinery rocked me, and fed me pills to make me sleep, and injected me with meals, and wiped away my tears with anodyne sponges.

"How kind of you," I sniveled to it, forgetting I had set the switches for this care, and wanting to forget.

The third night I dreamed I was in a great hall. Outside the hall stood people, not from the cities but from the desert, ghosts of the nomads that had wandered about there eons back. The hall had many tall windows, each of which was thickly curtained. But the curtains kept drawing themselves open, and then the nomads would intently gaze in at me. I went from curtain to curtain, closing them again, but as soon as I pulled one pair together, another pair would part.

At the hall's center stood a table with a flagon on it, and in the flagon, bright-blue wine. I knew if I could get to the table and swallow the sapphire liquor everything would be all right. But somehow, I wasn't permitted to drink while the people outside were watching. And the curtains opened and opened.

Finally my eyes opened, and I was awake.

A crystallize chronometer had been set going in the wall by one of the robots, part of normal sand-ship-run procedure. It wasn't on city time, but desert time, and it told me that among the geography outside, dawn had come.

I swung off the bed and stamped into the bathing unit. I splashed and brutalized myself under freezing jets, was dried and almost accidentally creamed, powdered, and perfumed by wild machines that leaped on me from the walls. In my cabin, a meal-injection, and four oxygen tablets downed in a pint or so of fire-and-ice.

I strode toward the forward end of the ship. Coming to the bank of switches, I almost wavered, but the dream had infuriated me. There was, after all, no sapphire wine of forgetfulness here. With a flailing hand I spun a dial, and thereby indicated to the ship that it must stop.

An immediate sighing among the motors. A soft shuddering. Presently, stillness, broken only by quiet settling noises. I stood there, as if waiting for the crack of doom.

Come on, doom's not in here.

Suppose, I thought, suppose I've stopped us right on top of an erupting volcano. But, of course, the ship would automatically have adjusted such an error, overridden my order, and dashed to a safer spot. No good trying to get out of it that way.

The doors slid back with a subtle hiss, as if trying to catch my attention.

No need, I was hooked already.

I looked out, and my legs turned to water, but I gripped the doorway and went on staring.

"Come on, *ooma*," I was burbling to myself, "you weren't scared before, you liked it before. How *derisann*, you said. Merely observe the majesty of the mountains, all black and jagged on the turquoise sky. Concentrate on the horizon, the color of those special rose sweets Thinta used to eat. And the sand. Go down and touch the sand. How *groshing* it is, isn't it? Come on, you bitch."

I tottered down the ramp and half fell, strengthless, on my knees. The sand felt dry and brittle, each grain separate and individual, pressed into my skin. The atmosphere also was dry and brittle, already hot from the risen furnace of the sun, and the rocks were blistering.

"No, don't look at the sun. Remember, you can't, not like a dome sun. Now, a bit at a time. Just start with the sand."

Air whistled around me. The planet appeared to spin in slow arcs that I could actually see and experience. When I lifted my watering, barely focused eyes to the horizons, the mountains seemed to tilt, about to collapse on me. The sand sifted through my fingers. The rocky ground beneath me, at least, felt almost stable.

Breathe shallow, remember, don't strain to get extra lungfuls: the tablets will take care of the oxygen. No, the mountains aren't falling, nor is the sky. I won't be beaten. No I *won't*.

Then I raised my head slowly again to face the land, and I screamed.

It was standing there, eight-legged, on a rock. Hardly a petrifying sight, obviously scared half out of its own probably limited wits. About the height of my kneecap, pale lemon in color, its fur standing out from its body like a brush in fright or surprise. Two gray eyes of incredible innocence and a chocolate ruff completed the enchanting picture.

My heart swelled. I'd forgotten the animal population of the desert. At BOO they trap desert beasts, attempt to train and tame them, and sell them in the Fours as pets. My pet had been such a one. More interesting and more trouble than an android creature, pets frequently run amok in the streets of the cities, biting all and sundry.

"*Attlevey,* beastie," said I, in the voice of a saccharine floop. I was trembling at the contact, at the live presence so near to me, when I thought I should never see or touch anything live again. How I ached to grab that ludicrous furry real body. "Are you hungry, beastie? Fancy a little snack? Wait there, pretty beastie. Don't go 'way."

Making the most absurd gestures of patience and supplication, I crawled backward, scrambled up the ramp and into the ship, and flew madly for the provision dispenser.

What would it like? Nut paté? Salad-on-ice?

I loaded a platter with messy, hastily prepared delicacies, and stole back to the doors. Would it have run off?

At first I couldn't see it, and desolate tears burned my lids. Then I spotted its lemon form, lying backward on a nearby rock, sunning its stomach, and looking at me upside down with pop eyes.

"Here, pretty, pretty. Come and try the nice first meal maker's brought you."

I recall, with nauseated shame, my antics. How I crept about on the sand, hoping to approach. How it bounced upright, eight legs set for retreat. How I fell back, apologizing.

I finally deposited the plate about ten paces from the ship, and removed my obviously leprous and unwanted presence to the doorway. Where I sat, motionless, watching.

Lemon-furred Gray-Eyes remained upright about half an hour, pointed nose pointedly in the air. Eventually, with a proud and aloof demeanor, Gray-Eyes pattered up to the food and began to eat. Pausing only once, when I ventured to congratulate it, to direct at me a look of disdainful warning: Shut up, or I go.

Witnessing Gray-Eyes golluping made me hungry, but I didn't dare leave the doors in case it was gone when I returned.

Soon the food platter was empty, and Gray-Eyes, having licked it pristine and turned it over to make sure there wasn't some other tasty bit of something on the reverse side, sat down and began to wash. A fascinating sight, particularly since none of the eight legs seemed terribly well co-ordinated with the others. Perhaps Gray-Eyes was very young, or perhaps it just didn't care.

When it rolled over for the ninth time, I laughed, which wasn't the thing to do.

Gray-Eyes drew itself to its full height—two feet?—made some sort of blood-freezing threat-display—bared gums, daft ears back, ruff bristling—and bravely ran for its life.

My loss at its flight was mingled with hilarity. I shouldn't have laughed, I knew it. But oh, the relief of laughter.

It wasn't till I had gone down to get the plate (charming with saliva, and slightly chewed) that I realized the desert had stopped rotating and the mountains tilting. I looked right up at the sky, beautiful arch of heaven high above. Agoraphobia had perished, along with the cactus-cream, in Gray-Eyes' silly little teeth.

There was something I wanted to say to someone. I couldn't think quite what, or to whom. Maybe one of those ancient rituals . . . prayers? But going in, stubbing my toe on a rock, it was other things I actually said.

3

So my love affair with Gray-Eyes began, and a stormy and tempestuous affair it was to be.

I'd only meant to stop to do battle with my phobia, and the place I'd picked was random, chosen blind and angry by the spin of a dial. Odd to consider how important the most haphazard and trivial of decisions can turn out.

Naturally, once I'd made contact with my visitor, I reckoned on staying put a while longer. I planned to win the little *thalldrap*'s interest and affection by stuffing food down its gullet until it was too fat to waddle off again to the Hard Life. Failing that, I was prepared for kidnap. To such doleful measures are the lonely reduced.

All that first unit I prowled the adjustable veranda I'd forced into constructing itself along the "porch" side of the ship, or wallowed on the pillowy couch I'd installed there just by the doors. A robot, programmed to bring me Gray-Eyes-tempting trays from the saloon, scurried back and forth. Absorbed in my scheme, and probably more than half *zaradann*, I gobbled things myself off the trays, watched magazines, and frequently cajoled the desert: "Come on, aren't you hungry yet?"

It never occurred to me, though it should have, with my previous experience on the archaeological site in the past, that something other than the expected guest might materialize, having sniffed the odor of victuals on the breeze. Luckily nothing did, for in the condition I was in I might well have accorded it equally friendly treatment, and got divided, devoured, and digested along with the meal as a reward.

I hadn't really looked at the terrain much: getting over my fear of its openness had been enough. In the desert, initially, everywhere is like everywhere else—sky, sand, mountains. So far, this was the extent of what I'd seen in my involuntary roost. Then the day began to ebb, the world turned to topaz and gold, and the color of the sky seemed to sink away into the disc of the sun. I found I really could touch

69

the beauty of it then, as I had touched its beauty so long ago when I was free to travel where I wished, and the city still owned me. Now, tinged with my sorrow, the loveliness was bittersweet, but strong as wine.

The ship perched on highish rocky ground, which in turn fell quickly away into a valley of dunes edged east, north, and south by the fabulous, many-shaped crags. None of these looked particularly violent, and the lava traces I was still able to detect, more or less at a glance, were absent from their lean, gnarled thighs.

The scent of the desert changes at sunfall, as it changes at dawn. This I'd forgotten, maybe only because I couldn't bear to remember in sterilized Four BEE. At early evening it's a smoky voluptuous scent, like a candle of incense burning down, but this alters, as the air darkens and the stars emerge, to a hollow, almost spiritual smell of emptiness. After the rains, the perfume of green oxygen fills the spaces, and inebriates.

I'd got up from the veranda, and wandered down and out into the dunes, a damn silly thing to do, as are most of the things I do, let us admit. Suppose something were to pounce—

Something did.

Gray-Eyes.

"Gray-Eyes!" I shrieked, and God, how that high female voice got on my nerves after three *vreks* of baritone alternating with silver tenor. Apparently it got on Gray-Eyes' nerves as well, for, leaving the steaming dish I had laid out for it but ten splits before, it fled.

I tore my hair and rushed for the veranda, yowling at the robots to fetch more food. It was too awful to have lost the wretched animal when I'd been waiting the entire day. However, I needn't have had such a fit. For no sooner had I collapsed upon my pillowy couch than Gray-Eyes reappeared, virtually out of nowhere, thumped up to the dish, and resumed work. Nevertheless, its rear end was noticeably tense. "I'm doing you a favor," that rear end said. "I mean, I don't really *like* this muck, but one doesn't want to be rude. Still, watch your step. It won't take much for me to bolt."

I cringed, quietly, eating up Gray-Eyes with my glance. Every twitch and burp was dear to me. I longed to cradle it in my arms. Let's face it, *ooma*, I thought, it's the only child-substitute you'll ever get, some poor little animal you've seduced out of the dunes with your filthy synthesized nut-meat.

One of my reasons for remaining a male so long had been that child thing.

I'd killed my child, too, hadn't I? Due, as the Q-Rs said, to sheer folly. They'd never, never have let me make another child, even when I was out of Jang. They didn't trust me, despite the fact that after my one mistake I'd hardly have fooled about in that area again. (That was the stupidity of their assessments, wasn't it? They could act on deeds, but not on psychology, the knowledge that you might have *learned*.) As a male, my paternal urge was around ten percent, very low. But when female, though only at certain intervals, the yearning came strong.

So here I was in the waste, female and childless and yearning. So watch out yourself, tiny lemon-fur, I'll make a pet out of you yet. And this time there'll be no shock wall, and no death for you. I'll wrap you in cloud cotton if I have to, I'll defend you with my good right arm.

4

Several units I courted Gray-Eyes by putting out sumptuous feasts. Dawn, noon, and sunset came to be the set times for feeding—Gray-Eyes, naturally, determined these times. Having fed, Gray-Eyes would wash thoroughly, presumably in order to scent itself with the aftertaste of syntho steak-jelly and liver-root. During these ablutions I was careful to observe a respectful silence. At last, the guest would lie down on the rocky slope just below the ship, eight paws pointing heavenward, belly distended, and looking at me upside down.

Always then I made the fatal mistake of trying to approach. Sometimes Gray-Eyes would let me get within arm's length before scooting away across the dunes—or into them, for I would soon lose sight of it.

Through the daytime, only too aware of filling in the hours, I went for brief trudges here and there about the sand valley. A modicum of caution had returned, and I didn't wander too far from the ship, never out of sight of it, and always I took a robot with me. I wasn't sure, in an emergency, quite what it would be able to do, for they carry no armament, of course. Still, perhaps, I could get it to sock any ravening monster on the jaw. My knowledge of local fauna was more or less nil. My most dangerous encounter formerly, I had to admit, had been with the ski-feet, whose worst fault might only have been that they'd trample you underpaw in order to sample your earrings.

The robots weren't meant for the outdoor life, though; they tended to get dust and rainbowy sand in their valves, and would suddenly stop in the middle of nowhere to service themselves with reproachful, martyred clatterings. Fortunately nothing attacked. In truth, apart from Gray-Eyes, and maybe other gray-eyeses, the valley appeared uninhabited beyond the odd pale furry snake, humping morosely from dune to dune. The watercourses in the desert were sunk deep, and rare, and none seemed present hereabouts, which probably accounted for the depopulation.

Nevertheless, I enjoyed my walks—falling down sand-slides, over rocks, into small faults. The air hummed with heat, and a few miniature hard-shelled insects, which dived about on tinsel wings, made strange faint whispery noises. They seemed indigenous, for I couldn't remember seeing such entities elsewhere. But then, how much *had* I seen before?

At night, the cool came. The sky was black, but outlined against the mountains, oddly phosphorescent. Stars dazzled. I'd already got a couple of landmarks—a northern crag that reminded me of a fire-apple (round and pitty, with a sort of stalk); another to the east like an enormous cup, its sides eaten inward by wind, sun, and rains, its summit widening into a large smooth overhang, which one unit, no doubt, would come crashing off and frighten me into a paroxysm— if I were still in the vicinity.

Then—about three hours after sunset, almost to the split—the Sisters would go off like two great guns to the south.

I hadn't been able to resist calling them that. Sisters and brothers were figments of the past, ancient history. In the cities, nobody was permitted to make more than one child per Ego-Life—that is, between PD sessions—so consequently nobody ever got a sister or a brother. The supposition of re-lated flesh from one's own makers had intrigued me when I read about it in the History Tower.

By day, the Sisters were very far off, blue and vague with distance, like two pillars of almost-blown-away smoke, about half a mile apart, and apparently identical. In the dark, lit with their own red glare, as they puffed up steam and the odd fountain of molten pumice, they had a suggestion of slender aggressive villainesses from antique romance, toss-ing their ruby hair. Lucky for me they were too remote to wreck the valley. At any rate, their nightly performance only lasted about ten splits.

Tonight I'm going to get you, Gray-Eyes.

The sky was turning cinnamon and green as I lurked on the veranda, dish of goodies in hand.

"Here, Gray-Eyes," I yodeled. "Come and have your lovely seventh meal!"

Gray-Eyes, you bet, was intending to do just that, and

came racing from the rosy dusk. However, no platter lay in the sand. *I* had the platter, I, Gray-Eyes' wicked stepmaker.

Emitting encouraging noises, I held the plate in Gray-Eyes' direction. Probably the rotten little *floop* would take to its heels. But no.

Gray-Eyes stole toward me with a sidling, anxious motion. "I know you'll slay me," its tragic gazes said. "But I've no choice since the skin is sticking to my ribs." Some ribs. It was already so fat it could hardly walk. I would have to diet the poor thing later or it would go off bang. Maybe the provision machine could rustle up some starch-reduced kidney-rissoles?

Now Gray-Eyes was on the veranda.

I backed, very slowly, into the ship, and set the plate down on the floor of the open general area beyond, between the steel pillars. Then I sat stealthily on a velvet seat, my hand on the switch which would shut the doors.

Gray-Eyes entered the ship with a look of unconcern and indifference. Obviously, Gray-Eyes fought dragons and conquered citadels in its spare' moments, *I* was the only thing which gave it nightmares.

Gray-Eyes reached the plate and fell to.

Then conscience smote me. With the ultimate power of capture in my grasp, I felt a positive slime-crawler, and took my hand off the switch. Oh, let the animal go free. I pictured it, a prisoner, sodden with fear, huddled pathetically under a table in the saloon, refusing to eat, refusing to move, pining away. My, my, was I in for a lesson.

Presently, seventh meal decimated, Gray-Eyes stationed itself, legs straddled on the mosiac, and began its washing procedure. However, the rite seemed rather shorter than usual, and was soon concluded. Next, Gray-Eyes rose, and glanced about for the first time.

Its eyes frequently goggled, thus it was hard to be sure if it were as genuinely madly interested as it now looked. But, after a brief sniff about, still goggling, it turned and headed for the interior of the ship, and my mood jumped a notch or so. Being very slow and careful, so as not to cause panic, I crept after.

Then Gray-Eyes reached the saloon.

And then it started.

A robot was laying seventh meal for me at the center table, and very nice it looked. Jeweled plates, crystal goblets.

The glitter perhaps attracted Gray-Eyes, or the possibility of further refreshment. Whatever it was, Gray-Eyes proved an opportunist.

The plates went one way, goblets the other, and the silver placemats discussed in four directions. One cought the robot in the thorax region, and presumably activated some metaphysical theory that if there was trouble, the robot was going to deal with it. It lunged about, registered the position of Gray-Eyes—currently unsuccessfully champing a fork on the rugs—and made a grab. Gray-Eyes spat out the fork, which shot into the table leg, and went into its threat-display, naturally to no avail. So it bounded for the wall drapes and ripped its way up them, and onto the latticework ceiling, and inevitably reached the large, decorative chandelier, which depended, glowing with chemical fire, above us.

"No, Gray-Eyes," I cried. "Naughty."

I'd always liked the chandeliers on the ships, but not now that this one was swaying in vast donging arcs, fortunately non-hot flames hailing on the robot and me and everything else, Gray-Eyes slithering and scrabbling at the center.

"Come down, Gray-Eyes," I entreated.

I pushed the robot to a spot where it could catch the flailing lemon bundle, but Gray-Eyes studiously avoided us, and toppled instead, frantically clawing, down a fresh lot of draperies, landing at the archway where the robot-kitchen lies, tastefully hidden behind crystallize automatic doors.

"No!" I yelled.

Even the robot made a noise—involuntarily, I think, some overstrained joint protesting.

But it was no good. Trailing clawfuls of shredded curtain and faintly shining with droplets of chemical fire, Gray-Eyes sped with hurricane force at the doors, which obligingly automatically opened, and vanished into the metallic jungle beyond. After which the doors *jammed*.

Some of the vandalized satin-of-gold had got caught between them, no doubt, hence the difficulty, but the reasons for the fault were my last worry. I shouted useless orders at the meal-robot and at the other robot that had come thudding in to help. They were trying to bash the doors down, unaccustomed to such catastrophes, and over their racket I could hear the sound of metal racks going over and ball-bearings or something rolling, and something else rolling, which was probably Gray-Eyes, and then a most terrifying silence.

Just at that split the doors unjammed abruptly and both robots fell through into the kitchen. I didn't stop to pick them up as they lay there threshing feebly among the steaming debris of Gray-Eyes' passage. Gray-Eyes itself stood precariously poised, with noncommittal lethargy, upon the brink of the chute which passes down into the bowels of the provision-dispenser.

I took the kitchen in one leap, but wasn't quick enough. With a nonchalant yawn, Gray-Eyes slithered from sight.

Down in there a whirlpool of—what? I didn't know, but my mind's eye supplied an amalgam of steel cleavers, pulverizers, mincers, pestles and mortars. Wailing, I flung myself upon the machinery. There was a little button, I'd seen it before, a little black button with an enormous red message printed over it:

TO HALT MECHANISM, DEPRESS ONCE.

WARNING! USE ONLY IN EXTREME EMERGENCY.

I stabbed at the button with both hands, and next instant the world went mad.

First off, the machine regurgitated Gray-Eyes at about eighty knots and covered with this evening's proposed menu —cactus-pineapple, cheesecake, the lot. This object, propelled through the kitchen doors, which had jammed open now, thonked to earth out of sight, and made its departure, stickily and fast (as I later deduced from pineapply pawmarks on the rock outside).

Post Gray-Eyes, there erupted from the provision dispenser about a hundred miles of leather-of-steel moving belt, plus a gallon or two of cold soup which promptly flooded the kitchen area and washed through into the saloon and beyond with liberated gurglings. This, however, was a mere divertissement compared to what followed.

Scarcely had I time to curse than an explosion cursed louder, from the guts of the ship where the lower tubing of the dispenser shared bow-storage space with the tanks of the water mixer. The whole ship, taking umbrage, bucked and writhed and seemed about to turn turtle.

Things previously undamaged rained about my ears; worse than earthquake, the floor wriggled queasily. Rugs, robots, furnishings, and I floundered among the heaving soup.

Then nemesis. A great whoosh, a wave of heat and a wave of cold, the ominous grumble of some force re-strained—followed by the splintering roar of restraint collapsing. Last, a bang to end all bangs as part of the roof of the sand-ship ejected into the night, oxygen compression whistled away, and a jet of combined semi-synthesized food and ready-mixed water arrowed northward at the stars, missed them, and crashed spent upon the recumbent desert.

5

"Help!" I screamed into the monitor beam. "Help! Help!"

Far off in Four BEE sleeping circuits presumably engaged, and the link awoke. A crisp sizzling on the frequency, followed by the cool, stern voice of the computer, interrogating me across the miles.

"What is it that you need?"

It was no good trying to be prosiac, up to my knees in soup with half the ship gone and half the alarms of the ship going off all about me, quite pointlessly, I might add.

"Need? Need? Can't you hear?"

"I can hear perfectly. What is it that you need?"

"Help. I told you."

"Help of what kind?"

"A couple of crates of roofing, a new provision dispenser, and—oh, dammit—a deaf-aid if this bloody row keeps up."

Clicks and whirrs greeted my gospel.

"I am afraid we are not quite clear as to the nature of your request."

"Listen, fool," I raged, "turn your recorder tapes on and record this. A desert animal fell down the chute of the provision dispenser and when I turned it off—the dispenser—something went *zaradann* and it's blown a hole in the bow of the ship. The oxygen is still pumping, but the concentration is none, since it's all leaking out of the roof—the hole I mentioned. And I've got a thirty-foot water-and-food spout from the explosion, which I assume means both the provision dispenser and the water mixer are totally *grakked*. And, as they're in the bow, that may also mean the drive motors are *grakked* up too. Thus, if you don't offer a friendly hand fairly quick I'm going to perish of starvation, dehydration, and oxygen deficiency. While static. What have you got to say to that?"

"Where is the desert animal?" asked the monitor computer.

That surprised me. Maybe it had my files in its little

brain-cupboard, or perhaps curiosity had overcome its reflexes.

"The desert animal has fled to its burrow covered in cheesecake," I said.

The computer ticked and tocked away. Reasonably, it inquired: "Your other option is still open. Do you wish to suicide and return to PD?"

"And save you the trouble of rescuing me? No, I don't. Just you tell those Q-Rs to keep their side of the bargain and get off their—"

"Here is an emergency robot-activator. Are your robots standing by?"

My three robots were actually still splashing around on the floor, but I thought they'd pick it up, so I said yes, and the code came through, all squeaks, howls, and honkings, which, coupled with the sirens and buzzers and warning bells, nearly reduced me to a permanent audiophobe.

However, it worked. About ten splits later the robots, reprogrammed to operate at maximum efficiency and with specialized orders to deal with the disaster, were pounding from stem to stern of the ship, setting everything to rights. Even the alarms were gradually turned off, and the soup began to withdraw its hold, leaving only a stray lentil, artistically draped.

"We have located your position, and an automatic high-speed repair bird-plane should reach you in one unit's time. You are advised to be alert for it. Till then, the robots have received instructions in the matter of food and water rationing and the temporary sealing of the ship. Defense and other mechanisms should work as per normal." There was then the slightest pause, after which the computer added: "We trust such an event will not be repeated. Desert animals should not be allowed aboard your ship."

"Balls."

6

An entrancing night.

An extra oxygen pill to be taken, which I was sure I didn't need, but it was robot's orders, and a temperature stabilizer installed in my cabin which hummed jauntily to itself. The pill made me lively even though I felt enervated, so I couldn't sleep. The stabilizer noise didn't help either, or the robots thudding and bonking about on the roof. They'd managed to stop the water jet, after a couple of hours.

The soup smell was evaporating, but not fast enough for the cleaning machines, which burst from the walls at irregular intervals and sprayed the ship with scented deodorant, and stuffed rags and itty disinfected brooms into every crevice. I began to prefer the smell of soup. At least it was quiet.

Finally I took refuge in the Transparency Tower, which, temperature unstabilized, was now freezing. But it was as far from the din as I could get. I glared out at the desert, wondering where Gray-Eyes was now. Probably licking itself silly getting off the cheesecake, maybe with a few friends in to help, telling them about the ogress in the funny moving house who had chucked our hero (heroine?) in a mincer, from whence it had only escaped by means of its cunning and gallantry. Doubtless it would be back anon with a hungry look, and then I was going to get a stacked plate of something and throw it right in its face.

Frankly, I thought the sand-ship the Committee had so generously given me had gone a bit to seed, for I'm sure others have had occasion to stop provision dispensers now and then, without such dire results. So, if they'd palmed me off with shoddy goods, serve them right that they'd have to send me succour all across the burning waste.

In the end I fell asleep in the chair in the tower, and had some exhausting overoxygenated dreams. In one, the sky was raining robot planes, each of which landed with a shattering bang. In another, a beautiful male emerged from the desert, a male from one of the old tribes, bronze skin and midnight hair, and swooned away at my feet with a piteous cry for water. And I, a calculating gleam in my eye, ran to get the aforesaid water, and of course the water mixer had exploded and there wasn't any. I was trying to force anti-dehydration pills between the unfortunate devil's tightly clenched and scowling teeth when the desert sun came up and woke me. And two seconds after the light touched my face, the Transparency Tower frantically opaqued, so I shouldn't see the frightening dawn. Though it was still there, outside; waiting for me? Well, at least there is always that, I reasoned sentimentally.

Fair dawn, always fair, so red, so emerald, so golden, bathing the sky behind the jagged silhouettes of the eastern mountains, and the peak I called the Cup looking just like a cup with pink Joyousness-type bubbly-clouds swimming over it.

So, without stopping to tidy up or go and inspect what the robots had achieved, for their dramatic hammering had ceased, I plodded to the outer doors, opened them, and went out to greet the morning.

The sun was already shining on my porch; below the rocks the unbroken sand looked like a carpet of pale jewels, except, I hazarded, bow-wards on the other side of the ship, where the spout of part-food, part-liquid had fallen yesterday.

The revolting fountain had angled northwest, and I couldn't see the disaster area from my southeastern veranda, for which I was thankful. I was staring up into the flaring sky, wondering if the super-fast robot plane might be early, when the revelation came to me.

It came coiling about the side of the ship, born on the dawn wind. It came like a rope of silver on the air. Green-silver. For a second I was dumbfounded, trying to place that unique and magic scent. Then I knew.

I tore around the ship, narrowly avoiding collision with a placidly ambling robot still intent on repairs. Tore round, and pulled up too fast and fell prone. Which was quite appropriate, for among the extinct nomadic tribes the prone position was the one in which they worshipped their gods.

The deluge of mixed water and semi-made food had covered about half a square mile of dunes. It hadn't lasted very long, maybe three hours all told. The rains, of course, which come only once in every three hundred days, and not even then necessarily, do at least last a whole glorious diluvian night. After the rains you could understand, even if you marveled at it, the extraordinary reply of the desert. But this.

Green shoots blowing like fine green hair before that morning wind. Green shoots thickly massed over half a square mile, like slender soldiery in some fable. And the scent of them, the smell of their sap, and the oxygen they expired. Some in bloom—little flowers or buds that might turn out to be anything, except that there wouldn't be time. The generating life of the sands, dormant, brought to fruit prematurely and by accident. And in an hour or so the sun would be draining the soul from them. By sunset they would be black and withered in this waterless place. By dawn tomorrow you could safely offer a prize to anyone able to detect their ruined dust among the other dusts of the land.

I stood and swore. I felt I had betrayed those shoots, dragged them up here on false pretenses without even a night of rain to sustain them, sold them out to the cruel sun. Dawn, *farathooming* dawn.

As I snarled there, along came a conscientious robot with a tray, and on the tray one meal injection (large), one draught of silver-cordial (small), six anti-dehydration tablets, four oxygen pills, and a lot of space.

"How *groshing,*" I remarked, knocking things back, and shooting things into myself ferociously. I balked only at the oxygen. "Look at that field out there; I'm not going to need these things. At least, not all of them." The robot whirred worriedly, and went into a tape-monologue-dehumanized voice stressing rather than alleviating solitude—about how I must take *all* the pills, *all* the pills. So I had to reprogram it quickly in the interests of peace.

When it had gone, I sat on the already hot rock, digesting my horrible first meal, and staring at the greenery. The idea arrived presently and was perfectly simple. No doubt anyone else would have thought of it eighty *vreks* before I did.

"Hallo there, it's me again," I informed the monitor computer jollily.

Quite probably it blew a steel gasket. It sounded like it.

"Wait. Wait," it chuntered out, and a wild rattling broke loose for a whole split before it had calmed itself down, or been calmed. Then: "There is no need to panic," it said. "The repair bird-plane is on its way, and will reach you at —click—click—computed time of desert sunset."

"Who's panicking?" I gravely asked, hoping it would get the point that of the two of us, *it* was. "I opened the link because I have another request."

"No other requests are acceptable until the first request has been granted."

"Nonsense," I said. "Suppose I'd broken a femur?"

"They are extinct," said the computer, either mishearing or, lacking certain vocabulary, making an uneducated guess.

"Listen, you," I said. "I'm an exile. Very well. But I'm positive that while I opt to stay alive, the Committee *has* to keep me that way. So if I say I need something *urgently*, you have to send it to me."

"We cannot send you any femurs," moaned the computer.

"I don't want a *drumdiking* femur, for God's sake."

It probably thought it was a femur that had fallen down the provision dispenser, but now something worse had slipped out.

"Godgodgod," it asked itself, searching frantically the stockpiled labyrinth of its brain. "Godgod? Godgod? Godgod?"

"Shut up. Cancel. Be quiet," I cried. "Forget about God. It's a sensation, a belief, I don't know— forget it. Forget about femurs, too. They're *not* animals, I've got a couple anyhow, and believe me, if I *do* ever break one, you'll hear me screaming quite clearly in the city without recourse to a monitor beam. What I want is this: one extra water mixer, on rather a large scale, about the size of the ship, say, and rigged for adaption, and some housing for it, and, obviously, self-servicing equipment tied in. And you'd better use a displacement machine, because I'll need it by noon at the latest."

There really was a sort of overcharge then. But the computer surmounted it.

"Why do you request this?"

"Because, my perma-steel friend, I'm going to make the desert waste blossom!"

The silence which followed was predictable and far from pleasing. But I stuck it out, knowing they had to listen, couldn't just leave me there; I'd got the Q-R Committee by their service-to-humanity-programming curlies. Though a menace, I was human, and I had a need, so—

The displacement machine had been an inspiration. It was a body displacer, of course, meant for people use, but since hardly anyone does use them because of the violent nausea that generally results, they are sometimes recruited for sending intercity hardware about. (Dematerialize on Angel Walk in BAA, rematerialize smack in Peridot Waterway, BEE, but that sort of mistake doesn't happen often, only when some Employed Older Person pops the wrong button.) If I could make them agree to my demands, BEE could shoot that water mixer out into my valley inside half an hour and, since water mixers are the stuff of life everywhere, it shouldn't be so hard to find one—or make one—by noon. Then, oh then—a nourishing rain could fall, and my garden—yes, I really thought of it already as My Garden—could go on growing, and, what is more, go *on* and *on*. If the desert yielded so verdantly after one night of rain, what *couldn't* happen here?

I was fired, ablaze with enthusiasm.

I beat the computer down—and the Q-Rs clustered by it now, I should imagine.

"I can't see a friend, can't even talk to a friend," I histrionically bawled. "Alone in the sands, and all I want to do is water a bit of *real* garden." (Boo-hoo)

There came at length a long long silence. From that silence, I knew I'd won. The computer spoke:

"For this item there will be a charge. You will have to pay."

I was het up enough at that moment they probably realized they'd get a mass of utilitarian energy from me, even on tape.

"Yes. Plug me in and I'll pay."

And I did. I gave them their water mixer's worth, and double. I sobbed and laughed and blessed them, and called down upon the city the joys of the firmament. It was worth it, and I didn't even know then how worth it it was going to be.

7

The paid-for water mixer arrived in the afternoon, with a low thud of displaced air. They'd aimed it at a spot about halfway along My Garden and just enough to the south of it to avoid crushing or smashing any of the growing stuff. The positioning was so perfect, I thought they must have made a mistake. They'd probably have liked to materialize the water mixer smack in the middle of everything, including me.

It was a big machine, too, everything I'd hoped for, and stylishly housed under an elegant ice-white cupola with pillars and steel-glass all about below, and doors that were set to open only to me or my robots. We wouldn't have any dear little desert animals barging in here, at least. The adaptors were excellent, too, and took my instructions like a miracle.

For an hour then, distant hummings and skitterings within the cupola, after which it finally happened. Vents swung wide in the dome, mother-of-pearl nozzles emerged like questing trunks, and fine, wide-spread jets of ready-mixed water began to fall, not only on My Garden but also on the dry, southwestern side of the water mixer, so perhaps I should be seeing another My Garden come up there as well, sooner or later.

I didn't know how much moisture would be needed, but the best method seemed to be, since it was intended as a long-term policy, little and often, with a rest by night for the machine to fix a fresh supply. (Water mixers synthesize their components from any rubbish to hand, and refine and intermingle them dextrously in the old water formula known even to the ancients. Anything can be made in this way, and it's a pity no one realized this fact before they'd completely drained the seas and the soil.)

Pride was not in it as I paraded the rocks around the ship, watching the "Rain."

See, *ooma* Garden, it wasn't a betrayal after all.

It was going to be about a mile west to north now, in addition to stretching half a mile from the ship.

Then the grand ideas started to come. Why not more? Why not My Gardens on every side, why not a valley of My Gardens? I might be able to get further water mixers from the city, if I confused the computer enough, or, failing that, get this one mobile, and wheel it about, doing shifts—two hours on the western land, two hours east, two hours south, etc.

Perhaps nothing would grow after all. The dunes couldn't all be so fertile. (Don't kid yourself, remember the rains—green everywhere.) And the valley was how big? An oval roughly, about ten miles maybe north to south, eight miles west to east. A tight schedule for one water mixer. But if it *were* all fertile in the end, all green . . .

Interruption to reverie was sudden and unexpected, though it shouldn't have been.

It was a laughable and terrifying sight.

Chugging along from the area obscured behind the ship, and making quite obviously for My Garden and the water-mixer housing, came what must be described as a tribe of Gray-Eyeses.

There were about twenty of them, all physically alike, except for grotesquely varying sizes—several were as small as a Jang girl's hand, two or three as large as a double float-bed. Demeanor seemed to accord with girth. The small ones tumbled and bounced and sometimes paused for boxing matches with each other till some adult (?) superintended them back into line. The big ones had a look of solemnity, even menace. The ones in between broke into fits of either mood, now stern, now downright balmy, clocking each other around the jowls, then striding on with a regal air, noses aloft.

Had they come to get me? What had Gray-Eyes Mark I been telling them?

However, they ignored me, though they knew I was there. (You couldn't miss the pointed way they sniffed upwind; it made me feel like dashing back in the bath unit.) What they were interested in, as I had first feared, was the rising of green.

Now what? Run into the Transparency Tower and activate a defense mechanism, something like the shock wall that had killed the pet? See their lemon bodies drop in ecstatic death, before they could tear up the precious shoots? No, I couldn't do that. Couldn't, couldn't and wouldn't.

Feeling stupendously brave in my cowardly way, I bounded down the rocks toward the procession, waving my arms and shouting: "Shoo! *Grak* off! Get out of it!" To which there was a thoroughly stunning response of complete uninterest.

I was almost on top of the Gray-Eyeses now, and dementedly picked up handfuls of sand which I flung over them. There *was* a reaction to this. A few of the smaller—younger?—Gray-Eyeses ran up and began to turn somersaults about my feet, which, despite everything, nearly undid my resolve to be fierce and adamant. And then a large one looked back, registered the action, and returned doggedly toward me. Now he/she would assume that I was massacring his/her offspring, or whatever they were, and floor me with one enormous paw.

"Help?" I asked experimentally. There were no robots in sight, naturally. "Look," I said tremulously to the advancing foe, "I think your family is *derisann*, but keep your feet off my blossoming waste, will you? And whatever you think I did, I didn't."

It reached me. I could gauge its size accurately now. It was exactly a head taller than me and rather more wide. Its eyes of deeply aqueous gray stared into mine, and it set its two front paws—compensating efficiently on the other six—upon my shoulder. Numb with fright, I stood my ground. They were quite light, those paws. At least it wasn't giving a threat display.

"Er," I said, "I only meant—"

Its mouth opened and a pale-pink tongue emerged, healthy and wholesome as a flower. It licked me.

Was it embracing me, or just using me as a balancing post? Why was it licking me so thoroughly? Its tongue was very nice, but I didn't really want my face washed with it. Was it getting the taste?

"So kind—*groshing*—thank you," I gabbled in a nauseating attempt to ingratiate myself.

Presently the licking stopped. I opened my screwed-up eyes and it patted me gently. Its paws left my shoulders. With one admonishing backward glance, scooping the little ones before it, the large Gray-Eyes went after its mates.

Feeling shaky with alarm, and laughter, I sat down in my tracks.

It was hopeless anyhow, they'd reached My Garden, and all was lost. Perhaps they wouldn't damage *everything*—

"Idiot," I said then. "Fool." Admittedly I'd seen what they were at. But I should have guessed long before.

They would never wantonly harm anything growing, except the really stable fixtures of the desert, which they used for food and then only sparingly. They had a respect for vegetable growth, it was bred into them, and not surprising. After the rains, they hadn't touched a thing, only danced in the lushest spots, had an orgy or two, played. And that was what they were going to do now, hold a post-rain rite. Because they thought it *had* rained, and somehow they'd missed it.

My Garden was going to be the scene of a celebration.

They wouldn't make a lot of mess, probably add a bit of home-grown fertilizer here and there. Would they be able to adjust? What would happen when they realized the "rains" and the plant growth were going on and on? Had I wrecked their ecological thingammy?

Ah well. Too late now.

A few more came in through the unit, Gray-Eyeses, and some insects, and a couple of snakes. It gave me a lump in my throat the size of a small mountain.

It was the robot rescue bird-plane, swooping in and breaking the sound barriers, that ended the ritual.

Gray-Eyeses and friends, sped, wriggled, and flew in all directions, and vanished like sorcery in the dunes.

A door opened in the plane and a machine rolled forth, robot voice-box patronizingly announcing: "Help is at hand," or something.

I tried not to glare as it began to fix my ship.

What can I say? How can I record the dream as it evolved everywhere about me, record it, and yet keep the dream intact? I could state every event as it occurred, every tiny and wondrous event.

The first bud opening, the first great ferns stretching for the sky, black-green on blue-green. Me bubbling like a *thalldrap* to one of my overtaxed, constantly reprogrammed robots: "I think this one's going to be a *tree*, a *real* tree."

Or there was the morning the sandstorm came, first like a golden gauze across the distant mountains, with Dopey staring admiringly at it, "My, that's pretty," until presently it smashed into us, wham, and flayed everything to within an inch of its life. Robots and me, swathed in bits of see-through to protect our eyes/optic circuits and lungs/chest valves, scurrying along between the slender irrigation canals we'd only just finished digging. (Brilliant notion gleaned from remembered antique manuscripts in the History Tower, these channels take water to the farthest reach of a plantation. They're meant to come from rivers, I believe, but we had to keep them filled from the water mixer. They were backbreaking to dig: I ached for ten units in muscles I never knew I had. The robots got stiff and fed-up, too, and needed oiling.) For about an hour we plunged around, tying things down and draping things over things, and six or seven times I trotted into the ship and shrieked down the monitor beam for a wave-net protector, which performance met with neither applause nor success. Luckily the plants, or most of them, nourished on so much liquid, withstood the storm.

Shall I mention the units I simply sat, watching the swaying green, or wandered through it, sometimes trailing the perambulating "Rain"? The water mixer plus housing had now been adapted for mobility, and followed its allotted course, looking most curious and spectacular, and from the distance, perfectly like some fabulous monster. A great gleaming white cupola, stalking transparent steel-glass legs, mother-of-pearl nozzles waving from its crown, spraying delicate mists of water, stopping at the newer areas for more prolonged sprays, then making inexorably onward. At night it returned to rest beside the ship, humming to itself as it made fresh tankfuls. It, too, was overworked. It could, in fact, despite my plans, patrol and moisten only a short distance from its daily supply north, west, east, and south from the ship, a round tour of about four miles. I'd need eight or nine more water mixers to realize a decent job of watering the arid wastes, and hadn't I just tried to get them?

"Your request cannot be granted," said the monitor computer, and said it again. And again. And . . .

"Found out what a femur is yet, dumb-cluff?" I infuriatingly asked it, and heard the poor thing go rattling off to itself. The routine never varied and I never got the water mixers. I once tried pretending the first had met with an accident—fallen down a fault or off a mountain, I forget—but they checked us via the monitor system, and discovered it merrily stumping about on the eastern perimeter of My Garden spraying efficiently, so that didn't work either.

Even those few miles, however, the sight and scent of them. Everywhere the water fell vegetation grew. A young forest was coming up to the east, and, starting just below the ship and spreading a quarter of a mile, tall, tall, slim trees, many-ridged trunks the color of dark jade and leaves thin as whips, strung like strips of green glass over the sky, making incredible patterns as they crossed and recrossed each other in the breeze. Flowers, too, every shade and hue, as the old books used to say. Some were climbing the veranda struts, and soon I wouldn't be able to move the sand-ship even if I decided to.

About thirteen units after the robot rescue plane had rehabilitated my vessel-home, a small avalanche took place over on the eastern slopes of the mountains, and the faintest of tremors disturbed the ground. Off went the alarms in the ship, and everything tried to dive for safety and found it couldn't, since I'd switched out the automatic drive.

When I'd quietened the sirens, I had to face a fact or two about the earthquake-prone terrain. I could stabilize the ship, mobile or static, but what about the Garden out there?

We'd begun to get quite handy and capable, the three robots and I. (I'd given them names by then, as I'd known I would, *and* programmed them to respond to them, *and* I chatted away at them, too, just as I'd feared. Still, it was eccentricity rather than desperation, and it had practical uses, for they came now at a name-shout, and if I told one to fix supper I could specify, and the other two—who might be hoeing with me outside or something—wouldn't fling down tools and charge off as well. They were known as Jaska, Borss, and Yay, the tags of three ancient chieftains Assule had once spoken of during the Archaeological Expedition. Assule had been a bore, but somehow the names stuck, maybe only because it was so boring: so Jaska this, and Borss that, and Yay the other. I think they were related or buried together, I can't recall.) Anyway, Jaska, Borss, Yay, and I, along with machinery borrowed from the ship, began to try to manufacture stabilizers of our own out of materials got from Four BEE under false pretenses.

I told the monitor beam how sad and *droad* I was. I said I was going to design a charming little tower as a hobby. Could they let me have some steel of something and silk of something else? Oh, and some weeny components, nothing much. I'd worked out that, so long as they thought I was up to something deadly, piffling, and useless, they'd let me do it, and I was proved right, for piece by piece, out came great crates of stuff for my "tower." I supposed they'd concluded that when I got purposeful about things, I also got violent, and upheaval followed, and I supposed probably they had a point. However, Jaska, Borss, Yay, and I got to work on the load, using one of the ship's stabilizers taken apart as a model, and, some units later, we began to dig holes and put down our first efforts. Only when disaster struck would I know if we'd got the formula correctly, but it *looked* right. I even wondered if we could build the extra water mixers ourselves, but it would mean stretching the tower-myth out rather thin, and also dismantling the existing mixer for a blueprint, and if any of us messed it up, we'd have no mixer at all. So, for the time being, a four-mile circumference of greenery it was going to have to remain. Anyway, that was fairly tiring.

Most days I went out with J, B, and Y and we turned over the soil—it really was starting to look like soil, too—and inspected growth, and tied weaker things to steel sticks, and made a note of where looked the most parched so the water mixer could give it an additional blast. Though the oxygen was invigorating even under the adolescent, burgeoning shade, it got very hot, and after a morning of it I would stagger off someplace and swoon away for an hour. Sometimes I would find a recumbent Gray-Eyes swooning there before me. I never knew if I met the original Gray-Eyes Mark I; it hadn't come to the ship again, certainly, which was, no doubt, as well. I was too busy to mourn or be glad at its absence, too involved in the project to be lonely.

My beautiful body got more tanned. I was the essence of dark honey now, and my fair hair bleached to milky amber with fiery streaks in it like decorative silver chains. The poet's eyes were two iridescent, almost colorless blue pools in that dark face. Mirrors made me jump even more, though a couple of exhausted evenings I lay on my veranda staring in one through the fading red charcoal of dusk. Sexuality hadn't been much of a problem yet. I was too worn out. The love machine had cobwebs on it, or would have if the ship's cleaners didn't burnish everything nearly skinless. Still, the reflection of the beautiful girl with the eyes of the beautiful young man I had formerly been induced in me a kind of sinuous excitement I was going to have to beware of.

Thriving on water, every day the growing green rose higher and stood more strongly. Forest leaves tapped on my cabin windows, which faced out now, for I'd replaced the brocade with glacia-view. My window gazed southeast, like the veranda. I could see the dawn come up like rubies and limes behind the serpentine trees. And, if I had gone to my couch, the Sisters generally woke me with their sullen guns and villainous red hairdos so far across the valley.

What can I say? Maybe not all that.

This is a kind of retaliation, isn't it, to that other screed of mine, composed in Limbo twelve *vreks* before in distress and query? That—the question. This—the answer. Or part of the answer, for all my life will be a reply, to myself and to my world.

Maybe, though, I should only say that a *vrek* passed by across my valley, a hundred units. And that one day I went out of the ship, and I saw everything with a kind of unexpected clarity, as if I hadn't seen it before, hadn't watched it grow, or helped it.

The sun was blazing down already, that cruel unbiteable sun. Black mountains cradled the valley, and a rim of glistening sand. Within that, My Garden, like a green smoke drawing nearer, and, as it neared, seeming a vegetable city with domes and towers, avenues and arcades, palaces and porticos, and a couple of Gray-Eyeses were running about in them, being careful not to tread on anything.

I was totally ready to cry, being, as I said, sentimental and a *floop*. Just then the monitor beam signaled me, a rare occurrence, so I packed away my emotion and went to investigate.

I had corrupted the computer too, so much was obvious.

It said only two words, but with such triumph, almost obscenely:

"*Thigh* bones."

8

First unit of my second *vrek* in the valley.

Me on the veranda eating melon pancakes, thinking lazily of the work we were going to do today, Jaska, Borss, Yay, and I.

Water mixer on the prowl, dimly visible through an early haze, now and again hidden by trees, ferns, shrubs. A confused snake courting itself in the grass about nine feet off. Nose to tail: "Come on, give us a kiss." The tail coyly refusing.

Then a familiar-unfamiliar sound in the sky, the snake going stiff as a ramrod, and I walking out and staring up.

Sometimes bird-planes had passed over, actually far to the west. Rarely did you catch their noise. Purely at random, I had established my haven well off the sand-ship and plane routes. This abomination, however, was directly overhead and presently swooping earthward.

Farathoom, and similar oaths. Watch out for the purple trees! (I had a name for everything—generally analogous. This saved muddle. Sometimes.) No, the purple trees had escaped barbering. The thing was going to land right in the cactus roses. It did.

Pancake still in hand, I thudded from the porch and ran to the plane. Very garish it was, and drizzling colored neons, but I didn't bother with that.

"Get the Infinity off my flowers, blast you! Look what you've done."

The anticipated robot voice came melodiously from the opening door:

"No need for alarm."

"I'm not alarmed. But you're going to be if you don't move that tin can of yours."

Just then the visitor emerged, a roly-poly machine, somehow conveying broad smiles, wires waving, lights popping on and off. It had Flash Center written all over it.

"Don't tell me," I said. "Some soup-brained *promok* spotted a fern in the desert, and mentioned it to some other

93

Older *promok* at a Flash Center, and now they've sent a reporting machine to collect some pulchritudinous flashes to be pulchritudinously flashed all over Four *flooping* BEE. Yes?"

"Oh, *yes*," chortled the flash machine, programmed by some incorrigible moron to sound like the worst type of human jolly. They probably thought the distraught Outcast would be glad to chirrup away to something human-sounding, however obnoxious.

"Well, old *ooma*, you can just hop back on your plane and go," I said, "before I turn the water mixer on you."

The flash machine looked uneasy somehow. Maybe it wasn't rustproofed.

"Oh, but please. Everyone's ever so interested. There's even going to be a special interruption to Picture-Vision, and a perma-film of all this put on for five whole splits."

That rocked me. The last time that had happened had been when—when—well, when? Ever? Surely the Committee hadn't thought this up? Perhaps people *were* interested, or some people. Perhaps Danor might want to know how I was making out. Or Hergal. Yes, I could just see Hergal, reclining somewhere, semi-ecstatic, with golden limber limbs elegantly stretched like one of Thinta's cats. He might even get romantic over me for half a split now I was in noncombatant female form. Thinta, on the other hand, liked me less that way. Possibly she would mutter something like: "I *tried* and TRIED with her. I did all I could. But she *wouldn't* listen." It hurt to think of them, but it was a pain I'd have to get used to. I couldn't always just shut off whenever some image of the city stole up on me. Sometime I'd have to face it. But part of me had warmed. I looked at the flash machine differently.

"Well," I said, "if you'll shift that plane over a bit, and let me do the talking."

"Of *course!*"

"And could you readjust slightly, and speak more in the frigid supercilious vein I've become used to with machines? Oh, and I'll need half an hour to get ready."

Vanity.

Oh, well, the first chance I'd had to be vain for over a *vrek*. Could be the last chance, too.

A good machine can rustle up clothing in fifteen splits if you know how to inspire it. I'd long since got out of wearing traditional Jang see-through in BEE, so I'd had lots of practice in the art. The ship clothing machine, left in the wall till now, nearly went *zaradann*, and threw off a gown of syntho-silk the color of fresh snow and embroidered with zircons. The cosmetics chute had fun, too, and tossed jeweled bottles of this and that at me with a disarming, child-ish delight. My feminine side had reestablished itself with a vengeance.

I emerged back into the outdoors, looking unbelievably glamorous and confident, eyelids enameled, earlobes span-gled, and even the calluses rinsed off my ringed hands with medicinal salve. This was how Danor and Hergal and the rest were going to see me, if see me they did. Prosper-ous, fortunate, desirable, happy. And out of reach.

"You have been three half-hours instead of one," stated the flash machine.

"Oh, good. You've reprogrammed to sound unpleasant. That's a relief."

"No I have not, but my batteries will go flat if—"

"If we waste any more time, so let's get going."

Full tour. Everything. They'd cut it later, anyway. Five splits! What could they show in five splits? Just enough, maybe.

Trees in a stasis of showering green, irrigation canals sparkling like crystal, the monstrous water mixer lifting on its legs and striding off, a solitary Gray-Eyes caught napping in the fern. Me, pampered and relaxed. Jaska and Borss digging Yay out of a subsidence. ("You'd better cut that." Bet they wouldn't.) Fruit ripening—no, I didn't know what it was, but as it had grown here on the north side where the original water-and-provision spout had erupted, possibly some of the semi-constructed food had taken root or whatever it did. I'd be testing soon to see if it was edible.

Eventually the flash machine asked for a speech. I con-sidered *"Vixaxn* the Committee," succinct and sincere, but decided if I really wanted any old friends to see this reel I'd better think of something else.

So: "I just want to thank the Committee," I said, dewy-eyed, "for being so considerate. I made a terrible mistake, as everyone knows, but, despite exiling me, the Committee has been the soul of good will and consideration."

"How about loneliness," the machine asked, abruptly brutal, "and impending age?"

"You can be lonely in a crowd," I said, "worse than out here. And age is something the ancients used to cope with, so I can cope with it, too, can't I? Besides, I've got a good half *rorl* or more before I need start worrying about that. I'm built to last."

When the flash machine had gone, it was rather quiet for a bit.

I tidied up the cactus roses, but they were tough, and their scarlet heads were soon raised high again. So was my sun-bleached one.

Finally I got on the monitoring beam and asked the computer if they would relay the flash film to me on my own Picture-Vision unit. After a pause the computer said yes, and then:

"Currently, bones are reinforced while the child is growing in the crystallize tank," said the computer. "So are teeth and nails. They no longer break."

"That's a relief," I said. "Are you going to drop this femur business now?"

The computer rumbled.

"What is God?"

"I can't tell you. Don't ask again."

"This word does not fit into my vocabulary."

"Nor mine. Don't worry about it. Get them to wipe off the tape or something."

Rattle, pattle, ping.

The film wasn't bad. I didn't understand then (how could I? Maybe I could have, should have) how un-bad it was.

The Garden looked wonderful. Unbelievable. What effect would that produce after the silk-of-glass flowers and jade ilexes of the city? And I, well, I looked as I'd wanted to: radiant. My speech was in, even the hint of diabolic irony I hadn't noticed had slipped through on the "good will and consideration" bit. Still, probably the citizens would just scream: "Ooh, nasty real rough trees with creepy-crawlies up them, and horrid Jang exile murderer much too brown, and never trust people who give themselves pale eyes, ugh!" And rush for the vacuum drift.

Peace be with you.

9

Ten days went by after the day of the flash-film. I had no reason to count them then. I went on hoeing and patrolling and inspecting, lying, as if dead, on the veranda in the cool of the evening, oiling J, B, and Y, and watching the stars budding in the night darkness and the shadows lying blue and purple along the spaces of the forest. The trees had continued to grow and were now about twenty feet in height.

The sun fell on the eleventh day, as usual, and twilight hollowed the sky, and the water mixer came swaggering home, folded its legs, and settled.

"Look at that *sky*," I said to Yay, squirting oil into him and feeling rather embarrassed by the intimate gesture. (Heaven preserve me from getting a crush on a robot in my solitary state. I call them all "he" already.)

Looking at the sky, however, I saw a cluster of footloose stars, and heard again that tiresome sound which could only be a bird-plane. Off course, presumably. Over it went, flying south, and very low. Then, quite suddenly, it landed just beyond the perimeter of the Garden, about half a mile away.

I jumped up, half troubled, half elated. More Flash Center film to be shot? Or had those surplus food supplies come in early? I was very impressed they hadn't sat down on the greenery. A glacia lamp of mauve chemical fire burned over the porch. I hooked it off and, attracted by diversion, began to walk in the direction of my mechanical visitor.

Not a long walk, following the useful little steel paths J, B, and Y had put down here and there. But I was to be met halfway.

A grove of ten-foot feather ferns rustled and parted. Shadows slid and dappled. Hard to ascertain form, even with the stars and my lamp. I ordered:

"Don't come on for a split, robot, particularly with a heavy load. Let me guide you, or else you'll go crashing into an irrigation canal like last time."

"*Attlevey*," someone said, soft as if the ferns had said it.

I nearly left my skin. The lamp fell on the path and bounced wildly like a lilac dune-frog into some bushes.

So I couldn't see her, even though I knew it was Danor.

Part Three

"I'm sorry, *ooma*," Danor said, "I didn't mean to shock you. But I wasn't sure what else I could do."

I tried to say something, but my teeth were chattering too much.

"I remembered you aren't male any more," Danor continued soothingly. "And we—I won't impose on you."

"D-D-D—" I tried feverishly. Oh, God, get a grip on yourself. "Danor," I grimaced.

"Yes?"

"Danor, you shouldn't be—what are you doing here? Isn't there some sort of Committee bar on anyone visiting me?"

"Oh, yes," she said, so quietly only the greater quietness of the desert made her audible. "According to their records, no human must visit an outcast. If they do, they forfeit their right to return to the cities. They gave everyone a talking-to after you left."

"My dangerous tendencies, rubbing off on you, contagious, like a sickness . . . forfeit rights to return . . . what do you mean? Do you mean—?"

"I mean," said Danor, "of our own volition, we've made contact with you. Because we don't intend to go back to the cities." Very feminine and not at all coarsely she added: "They can stuff them right up."

I wasn't sure if the feeling in my chest and throat was nausea, tears, or nervous asthma.

"Oh, Danor, what an idiot. Get on your plane and get going. It's all very well, I've got some sort of ambition out here. But it's still rackingly lonely. Oh, get on your plane. Say it malfunctioned and you never meant to land. Say you spat in my face—horrid, antisocial freak that I am."

"Don't be silly, *ooma*," said Danor. "I wouldn't dream of saying it. Neither would—" she broke off, and through my panicky emotion I became aware that she'd broken off here and there before, and that some of the related actions had been plural.

"Neither would whom? You're not by yourself."

"No," she said. "He has a private bird-plane. We can live in that if we have to. We don't want to crowd you, or make you feel any obligation. It's our own decision to come out here. We can move off over the mountains, if you'd rather."

"You still didn't say who," I said.

"Kam," she said. "Who else?"

She spoke his name, not in the way I'd heard her use it before, as if she had lost him forever and learned to exist with the fact. She spoke his name with a sort of exultation, not possessively, but rather as I had said, only half an hour before, "Look at that *sky*."

And then, despite the unprecedented situation, and the amount that hung palpitatingly upon it, despite the fact that, as a female, I felt nothing sexual or even romantic for Danor, a pang of scorching jealousy went through me. A compound of many things, no doubt, recollected male pride in my lovemaking with the specter of Kam, who held her before me, hovering in the air; the fact, too, that no chosen male had followed *me* into the waste, no one had been near and dear enough to consider it or be considered.

"Shall we walk on, to the plane?" she asked. "Will you come and meet him? I came alone to try to lessen the fright I'd give you. How are you, *ooma?*"

"Simply *derisann*," I grated. *"Groshingly, insumattly* marvelous."

She lowered her eyes—lavender eyes, designed expressly to please Kam.

"I'm sorry," she said again. "You must think us terrible. We *did* see the flash-film. I think everyone saw it. But truly, *ooma*, I'd thought of this before. And we won't stay if you don't want us to. Even though you've made this place so lovely."

An impulse in me told me to reiterate my warning to go, not merely from concern now, but from irrational malice. But, shaking to my soul, confronted even by two people to be jealous of—two *people*—I said hoarsely:

"Yes, all right. I'll meet him."

The whispery insects indigenous to the valley had long since made a home deep among the green, and by night their dry rustling filled the avenues of the Garden. Starlight flecked the paths and faceted unreal tourmalines to spark among the leaves. Once Danor's eyes suddenly flooded with tears—something beautiful she'd glimpsed, you could tell. She said nothing more, afraid I should censure her cowardice in not risking everything till she saw what could be done with the dunes.

Parked on the southern perimeter, lights beaming, the birdplane was blue and modest.

Danor went up the ramp before me. She called out nothing to him, simply stood there, then turned and smiled at me. That smile. It would have looked silly and sugary on anyone but Danor, but she gave it a sort of genuine gleamingness, or perhaps her authentic passions did.

The plane, though smaller, was rather like that of Lorun, my sometime lover from Four BOO, everything laid on in miniature as it were, float-bed, bath unit, little provision dispenser. Of course, I was peering about at it, avoiding looking into the shadowy area of the control panel where Danor's Older Male was sitting.

"This is Kam," Danor said, introducing us politely. So I did look at him then. I felt disproportionately disagreeable, as I mentioned. The whole thing had thrown me flat on my nose.

"*Attlevey*, Kam," I said, making a big thing of the Jang slang—Danor and me sweet young Jang, him elderly decrepit gentleman.

He wasn't, naturally. He looked scarcely older than either of us, since bodies are all made youthful unless otherwise requested by the Older Person in question. Only in the eyes and the way he moved his face—his expressions—could you see the extra years, the Experience of Life. And he was a handsome bastard, in true style, smoke-dark hair, smoke-blue eyes, tanned like a beautifully varnished smoky bronze. Which made everything much worse. He was the first male I'd seen for one hundred and something days, and he belonged—every square inch, you couldn't miss it—to my friend Danor.

So now I was jealous of both of them.

Yippee.

"Saw the film then, did you?" I inquired. He'd said nothing yet. He smiled too—what a smile that was, maybe he couldn't help designing himself to be so attractive, but he could try and tone it down a bit for my sake.

"Yes. We saw the film together."

"Oh, together. Surprised you made the time to see films."

He laughed. Not at me, with me. Showing me I'd cracked a joke, and if I'd only get off my arrogance kick I'd be simply _super_ company. I frowned unbecomingly.

"After you left Four BEE," Danor interpolated, "we disintegrated rather."

"Poor things. It must have been absolutely awful for everyone, stuck there in the dome, and me out here in the middle of nothing and nowhere with nothing and no one—" I stopped just before the self-pity, creeping up under a cloak of fury, got me by the ears.

"Yes, we were selfish," Danor said, "and very, very frightened. Up until you actually left, everyone kept going by being angry and fulsome, and having a mad time—like the party. But on the fifth unit . . ." She stopped and her face was pale, so pale it took me back into that Committee room when she had stood there, palely answering the Q-R's rotten probings about Kam and her, her hands trembling. She hadn't wanted to be there and answer them, but she hadn't had much choice after I'd done over Zirk in the park. After all, it had been my own fault, hadn't it, throwing around challenges, getting violent, blaming everybody but myself.

I sat down on one of the rather pleasing midnight-blue seats.

Danor didn't resume talking. I could feel Kam looking at her, her looking at Kam, and great mutual gusts of sympathy for me passing between them.

Let's face it, he hadn't jumped down _my_ throat for screwing his lover the moment his back was compulsorily turned by BAA Committee. And he had more rights than me, sniveling little predominantly female fool.

"Er, would you like anything?" he quietly asked.

"Don't be kind," I said, "or I shall smother the upholstery with tears. Maybe Danor could go on with what she was saying, and I'll try to keep my ill-natured trap shut."

"Oh, _ooma_—" said Danor, but Kam must have shaken his head, telepathically advising her to do what I said. They really were a pair, just like lovers in old books—one mind, one heart and so on. They'd have made you puke if there hadn't been that sense of something shining and rock-hard at the spine of their idyll.

Danor went on in a light matter-of-fact voice.

"First of all, Hergal went and crashed on the Zeefahr again. We thought he'd given that up, quite a surprise. She—Hergal—came back a girl, and rushed off in a dreadful state with some other-circle Jang male to BAA. The male resembled your last body, *ooma*. It was sort of funny and sad. Thinta just shut herself in her green palace with swarms of cats. Mirri and Kley looked frightful. Mirri finally booked into Sense Distortion. As for Zirk, she got cut out of the circle. She was going around and around the city, female, with about six enormous other-circle males, and half the time saying she was someone else. So the Committee are on to her for Evasion, since paying for home and various other things in another name doesn't count, apparently. And Hatta looked unbelievable the last time we met."

"Utterly *drumdik*," I managed. "I can imagine. Eight black eyes, four yellow ears, and a tail."

"No," said Danor, "that's just it. Female, and beautiful."

Even in my arrested state, this registered. Hatta—only once had I known him to be beautiful, and never female.

I'd looked up by now, and shown some signs of incipient animation. Kam had popped a button somewhere and cool glasses of a non-Jang white alcohol had appeared. I drank, cautious at the shared, unknown but tasty liquor. Was I going to forgive them their naive and unkind arrival, all glittering with their love?

"Yes," said Danor, "Hatta as a girl is riveting. I don't know what she felt; she never spoke of it. But obviously she was making up for lost time. She was marrying male after male —generally two or three a unit."

"Oh well," I said, feeling dreary again in my mateless condition, "good for Hatta. And what about you?"

"I sat in your palace," she said. "I kept thinking about you. I know how stupid and useless and selfish I was. *I* hadn't been exiled, you had. But, *ooma,* I couldn't help it. People said you'd suicide and come right back to PD, but I knew you wouldn't, not after what you'd told me—that dream. The desert was—*part* of you? I'd known that somehow from the very beginning. Do you remember the Archaeological Expedition? I thought it then. I thought you'd find some wonderful buried fortress or something, and stay in the dunes, oh, *vreks*. When you spoke about it, the sand was blowing there, behind your eyes."

"She won't believe you if you put it like that," said Kam.

He might have read my thoughts, too—though I hadn't balked at the words as much as I would if someone else had offered them. Danor wasn't artificial. If she said she'd seen sand blowing behind my eyes, she meant it. And really, I knew what she meant, too. It stirred me, scared me, made me want to run out and start up the hoeing or dig another irrigation ditch.

"I believe her," I said. "No doubt you understand why I believe *her*."

He nodded, a little embarrassed suddenly, becoming aware probably of how they paraded their feelings without meaning to or being able to do anything else.

"But then," Danor said, "Kam signaled me."

"Ah ha," I said, "just like in an old romance. I might have guessed."

They both blinked, but, having got them both off balance, I didn't feel spiteful any more, rather protective, really. Though they hardly needed my protection.

"I gather," Kam said, "you know about the earlier business."

"I think we both know about each other's business in respect to Danor."

"Ah. Well. Maybe."

"To recap," I said, "the Committee in BAA fed you a whole lot of indigestible rubbish about you being bad for each other."

His eyes abruptly glinted.

"Don't be tactful," he said, "or I'll smother the upholstery with tears." Danor giggled. I found I had too. Oh, well. "The Committee actually said I was messing *Danor* up, so I cleared my unhealthy carcass from her path."

"And then, despite many experimental love scenes with *groshing* older ladies, the nagging pain continued in your heart," I said. They gazed at me. "Meanwhile, back in Four BEE, Danor wandered pale beside my pool in the deserted palace. And then. Hark! A signal popping and winking. Danor sadly switches on the image, and there, or here, is her lover. With screams of joy they greet. Well," I added slyly, "you did tell me not to be tactful."

"That's all right," said Kam generously. "You're not far out. The screams from my end were somewhat deeper.

Otherwise . . . I asked her to meet me in BEE; my boat was due in four units."

"When we met," Danor said, "we just went back to where we'd been before, only rather furtively. Kam really did pretend to be my maker half the time. I think Hergal guessed. Just before she fled with her new marriage partner, she kept on about you when you were a male. I think Hergal was more distressed than any of us. Isn't that odd?"

"Peculiar," I agreed.

It transpired that finally the idea had come to Danor—ignore the Committees and fly the cities, and live for love in the wild. They'd just come around to the notion when my film was flashed out. It made a sensation—which it hadn't been meant to, at least not in the way it did. Possibly the Committee had allowed the film in the hopes that I, emaciated and dolorous with despair, would provide a nice extra example of what unsocial tendencies got you. Or possibly even, if I looked fairly healthy and jolly, people might stop worrying and debating about me, and get on with the *droad* city round. But—

"Half the Jang went running about on the mono-rails immediately after," said Danor, "screaming and shouting. There were sixty-eight sabotages of the dome that night, and sand and volcanic ash and a couple of earthquakes got through. About forty Older People went crazy as well, and got roaring drunk in your honor, and drove the Q-Rs mad at Ivory Dome saying they wanted to get married to each other."

"A historic evening," said Kam. "In the morning the Committee signaled Danor, informed her that she and I had been registered as together once again, and must part for our own sakes."

"So we said we were leaving," said Danor.

"At which the Committee," said Kam, "accused us, in a most extraordinary tone, of planning to join you in dangerous, out-dome, anti-city activities, and that, if we left, it would be assumed we also wished for permanent exile. Like you, we could expect aid and supplies, and like you, we could expect to remain outcast until natural death placed us at the Committee's mercy for PD."

"God," I said.

Kam looked at me.

"That's a very old concept."

"So is the concept of androids working *against* people.

But it sounds to me as if the Committee is boiling all over its electronic brain casings."

"Quite," said Kam.

"So why ever did you come?" I asked, breathless (breathless and girlish beneath these charming eyes I would have to accept as paternal or fraternal). "Knowing—what would happen."

"I said they could be damned," he told me, "and Danor said much the same, with a few colorful Jang adjectives thrown in. Because I want her with me, and she wants me, and if the only way we can have each other is by leading what, after all, used to be a perfectly normal life, then that's the way it's going to be. If you'll befriend us, you've got a willing pair of hands for your greenery out there, two pairs, in fact. If not, and we realize you might rather not, we'll go and try to get something started elsewhere, the way you have. The growth rate of vegetation in the desert is phenomenal, which has always been known, and accepted, and entirely ignored by everybody but yourself." He was really getting going. I loved watching him. Better to have a crush on Danor's Kam than on a *flooping* robot. "I admire the way you've organized this," he said to me, and I glowed, choosing to forget the fact that almost everything had occurred as a result of accident, mismanagement, and idiocy on my part. "I'd like to help, and Danor would. And I'll tell you something else. Four BEE blew to the skies the night they showed the film. There are going to be others coming out here, too. Plenty of them."

2

Naturally, I told them to go. Go on, I said, who wants the company of sweet-natured girls and delectable males, both of whom praise me, and offer help for hearth and land, and promise further comrades to come, and who make me laugh and want to hug them sick? Well, obviously, I didn't do any such *zaradann* thing.

We sat a long while over our white alcohol in Kam's bird-plane. We got a little drunk and made drunken plans. I said they must come and live on the ship, for now at any rate. Plenty of cabins, I said. All colors of the rainbow—yellow, scarlet, apricot—but maybe they'd better have the violet one, it would tone with Danor nicely. And they'd be able to insist to Four BEE that they have a water mixer. Two, even. One for the home, one to make shrubbery. The Committee, if they hadn't denied it to the Outcast Killer, surely couldn't deny *them?* Naturally, they'd have to move out of my vicinity temporarily, in case the Committee monitored their position. (A beam had been installed compulsorily on the plane, so they could call for aid, etc.—or was it to spy on their activities?) While we were in proximity with each other, the Q-Rs would tell us to share my water mixers, but if Danor and Kam were over the mountains at the time, the city must deliver. Then, once the goods had arrived, my guests could return, plus water mixers, and we'd have three lots of "Rain" for the Garden. This seemed very logically worked out, and rather sharp. Kam congratulated me again on being devious.

It got latish, and suddenly the Sisters went off with their usual thump and the unopaqued windows pulsed with distant red. I'd been impressed by the windows and the arrivals' lack of phobia. Love had sustained them? They didn't jump much, even now. However, reaction to the Sisters expressed itself from another quarter. From somewhere aloft exploded Danor's swan.

I'd forgotten the swan, and so had they, it seemed. Perhaps

107

they'd slipped it something to keep it quiet on the journey out. Currently awake, it raced gawkily for the exit, and fled from the plane. Once outside, it burst into klaxon sneezes. Probably it had a pollen allergy.

Danor was concerned, and Kam practically helpless with laughter; I somewhere between. It looked as if the swan might well be a child substitute, too, for Danor, since she and Kam could never become makers in the city. Recalling my pet, and the horrendous adventure with the devil of the provision dispenser, I eventually sympathetically followed Danor down the ramp, out into the night.

Danor called to the swan across the dark, intermittently volcano-lit spaces of the whispering Garden. In reply, from odd nooks, eyes sparked gray (Gray-Eyeses, obviously) or gold (snakes). The swan meanwhile could be heard faintly klaxoning to the left and plodding stolidly over everything growing at ground level from the sound of it. I recalled that old fear of mine—that real desert animals might attack an android version, outraged at it for its weird similarities and differences.

"Danor," I said, "I'll get it; I know the paths," and shot into the undergrowth.

I was going quite fast, despite Kam's alcohol, when the klaxon ejections abruptly ceased, but right then I spotted the swan.

It was lying full length, swan-fashion, on the earth, and, for a second, I thought it was dead, and nearly let out a screech of primeval woe, as once before, so long before, yet clear as yesterday. More clear. The pet lying dead, and I—

But no, the swan wasn't dead. It was lifting its brainless, elegant head, rubbing its neck on the stem of a tall flowering cactus—thankfully not of the prickly variety. And now the swan was rolling on the cool, water-mixer-moistened soil. Its plumage was filthy already and it had petals stuck all over its beak. But unmistakably it looked glad, in the throes of genuine haphazard pleasure.

I hefted it under one arm with difficulty, and took it back to Danor.

One hour later she and I had it in the bathing unit, flapping and flailing, as we rinsed our future from its lavender quills.

3

The bird-plane took off in the morning. Watching it go, even knowing they would be back, something shivered in me. But I put my stale fright aside. I wasn't going to be alone any more. Danor and Kam, and others, plenty of others, so Kam had said. My head was ringing with elation.

They planned to put down just on the other side of the nearest ridge eastward, signal BEE on their monitor-beam, and let fly with all the jargon we'd thought up for the water mixers. Then Kam was going to adapt it—or them—as I had done, merely a matter of reprogramming them.

After that the bird-plane would return, followed at length by one (or two) water mixers, striding like terrifying beasts from a myth across the mountains into the valley. If Kam could inveigle the computer, as I had done, into using a displacement machine for delivery, the whole thing could be over and done by sunset tonight.

Tonight I would dress for company. So I spent about an hour during second meal with the clothing machine, arranging for smoke-amber satin-of-glass with amethyst fringes. Most becoming. The cosmetic machine could do my hair too, curls and coils and pearls and things.

The swan had gone with Danor, blessings on it. Last night it had rolled right over some fresh young flowering shoots, which had somehow survived. Yay and I did our usual tour in the tracks of the water mixer. We wound up on the northwest side, examining the curious earth fruits, which were now ready to be picked and tested by the food equipment for edibility. Of course, they might be poisonous or nontoxic but foul. Still, they looked nice, succulent red and yellow, and some little green crispy leaves in huddles, a sort of sand-lettuce, not to mention the bizarre, gold-freckled, dark tubers swelling in the shade. Borss and Jaska staggered into the ship with armfuls of stuff to set the testing in progress.

The sun was high and hot by now, the sky the hard deep

turquoise of noon. The mountains were like carvings from night left behind at dawn, the edgings of sand like powdered silver. And here light was raining in dapples of golden green through the tall trees. The trees were rising in avenues; there were glades and beds of flowers, as if the Garden had actually been designed, as if someone had left the seeds ready, buried in the dunes, formally laid out, each held in a dry time-pod until there should be enough prolonged water to break the spell and wake them. What an idea. Had someone? Some ancient, eccentric, brilliant ancestor of the cities, long before even the nomads violently trudged the waste?

Cogitating, up to my eyes in soil from the fruit picking, I suddenly heard the thrumming of a bird-plane, and looked heavenward. Danor and Kam back so soon?

No. This one was coming from the west. Coming roughly, perhaps, from the direction of Four BEE.

Off course, or playing air games. It would pass over.

A black speck in the burning green-blue sky, it resolved itself swiftly, showing its underside, dropping by hectic degrees. Someone was fiddling with the controls. Or, nervous, had screwed up the robot programming.

The plane swiveled slightly, and all at once dived. Instinctively I ducked, without real cause, as the vessel sliced the atmosphere above the trees. Was it going to crash? And on my prickly-fire bushes?

At the last possible split, the plane righted itself and flopped into an offhand landing in the grove of purple trees, about a hundred yards eastward.

I had been leaning on one of the metal things the robots rustled up to serve as hoes. Now, hoe in hand, soil on face and in hair, and combined interest, alarm, and ferocity in my glance, I made toward the belly-flopped plane.

They'd brought down some of the boughs, I furiously noticed, furious as a maker whose child has been bopped on the nose. Don't tell me, the *Garden* is now a child substitute. The plane, however, appeared intact, its door stood open, and a wild din was emerging, a din you couldn't actually hear.

Upper ear. Jang high-tonal-music tapes.

I reeled, swamped with giddy delight, scowling, and burst up the ramp into the plane, looking neither left nor right. I found the tape control instantly and, with the practice of *vreks,* smashed the button for silence. The mind-blowing

horror receded. Shaking myself like a Gray-Eyes which has
accidently rolled in some cactus, I glared about.

"*Attlevey*," voices murmured, silkily, joyfully.

The tiny plane, built to carry two, or three at the most,
was crammed with five Jang. Their hair was shades of yellow,
hyacinth, viradian, pink-orchid; the two females had long,
long nails, the males' nails were even longer. They wore
see-through, chains, rings, bracelets, anklets. They were smoking incense through tubes from a weeny glass bubble fixed
in the ceiling, their eyes were dark with ecstasy, and full
flagons of Joyousness were clasped in their pretty paws. They
smiled up at me from their semi-recumbent positions on the
couches or each other, and their sequined faces were full of
visions and mysteries, and shone with the pure radiance
which only total imbecility can bring.

Oh. Beautiful.

"*Attlevey*," they reiterated. A male with flowing dark-
green locks waved his hand.

"I'm Naz. This is Felainnillaloxiandphy."

"Oh yes," I said.

"We know who *you* are," he said.

"You do."

"Oh, *ooma-kasma*, we do."

I shrank. Effusive turd.

"Well, *ooma-kasma*," I said, "I really think you actually
don't, or you wouldn't be here." A cold anger, not untinged
by blind panic, had welled in my reinforced bones. "Just tell
me, have you informed the Committee you were coming
here?"

"*Ooma-kasma*," drawled Naz, popping an extra pill down
his gullet, "we went right in the Committee Hall, and oh infinity, did we like anything tell them. Listen, you *thalldraps*,"
went on Naz, demonstrating, "you can all jump in the
vacuum drift. We're off to where everything is for *real*.
You bet."

"So they know you're here. What did they say?"

"They said: If you go you can't come back—oh—if you go
you can't come back—oh—" Naz discovered he had
broken into an involuntary but apparently Naz-pleasing song,
so went on. The other four, Felainnillaloxiandphy, joined
in.

So there they were, a parcel of useless Jang idiots, entirely enmeshed in Jang mores and habits, intent on molest-

ing my desert. Did they really realize what they'd done? That they *had* been exiled? "For real. You bet."

"Do you have any link with the city?"

"Four BEE? Oh, yah, yah, *ooma*, my *ooma*. They put in a monitor beam in case we need any more ecstasy or incense," Naz broke off his singing to reassure me. "Say, *ooma*, have a pill?"

"No. Get on your beam link and tell the computer you didn't mean it. You want to come back."

Naz broke off again. Something had penetrated.

"But we *do* mean it, *ooma-kasma*. And we *don't* want to go back."

"Yes you do. Have you looked out yet?" Their windows were as opaque as their brains. Maybe they'd get agoraphobiafied and throw up all over the grove, but at least they'd leave afterward. How could the Committee refuse them reentry? After all, they seemed model citizens to me.

Inspired by the suggestion, they were scrambling about, agile and luminous, and nearly trod me under their sparkling feet as they dashed into the great outdoors.

It was worse, much worse, than I'd thought.

Not a trace of insecurity or fear.

They were wandering from tree to tree, flower to flower.

"Oh, *ooma-kasma*," they were extolling each other, "just look at this, and this. Infinity, it's all so *groshing*," as they squashed flat the buds and picked the newborn blossoms to stuff in their abysmal hair.

Maybe the Gray-Eyeses would get them.

Maybe the snakes would strangle them.

Maybe the food tests would prove the fruits were poisonous, and I could feed them to the Jang: "Computer? I'm afraid I have five Jang here, suicided, ready for PD."

They were swaying and swerving in the direction of the sand-ship, holding hands and pulling off leaves so they could admire them better.

"*Ooma-kasma-maa!*" they warbled back to me.

"Coming," I grimly answered.

4

They but *loved* the ship. They'd never been in one before. They dived into the cabins and out of them. They flung open the doors to the pool-tank and dived into that and came out soaking wet. Two of them, the two females—Felainnilla— got hold of Yay and tried to dismantle him, with yipping recollections of previous city dome sabotage. Having stopped this, I found the other two males—Loxiandphy—had programmed a machine for some sort of bright mauve paint, and were painting with it all along the tasteful walls of the corridors things like THE DESERT WASTE IS COSMIC, *OOMA* or CACTUS COME AND EAT MY SOUL. They weren't too hard to deflect, being smashed to the very small back rooms of their tiny minds.

At last they flaked out in their entirety in the saloon, and I got clearing-up operations under way. I glanced in on the food tests, hopefully, but the poison analysis wasn't complete and, in any case, looked as if it might be negative. Perhaps I could grate some syntho-something in their fifth meal.

For they'd ordered fifth meal from Borss, and it had come. Tucking in with good appetite, they bawled away about how wonderful it was to rough it in the wild, so clean, uncluttered, and fresh, *ooma-kasma*. Then a male with hyacinth tresses (Loxi) and the female of the pineapple curls (Felain) went rootling by on their way to clash nastily with the scarlet cabin. I just knew they'd very carefully married before they left BEE. Unable to resist having love in these bucolic surroundings, the dust-pink Nilla girl and Phy, a grim, macabre cobalt creature with jewelry to match, thudded out to the yellow cabin. Naz lay among the debris of nut-steak-on-fire and smiled in laconic fashion.

"Well, *ooma-kasma*. I know you don't believe marriage is necessary first, so what about it?"

I still had the steel hoe in my hand; I showed it to him.

"I've been male enough times to know just where to aim so

113

that it hurts," I said. "Until I can get you off my patch, I realize I'm stuck with you, but don't push your luck."

Even I was not that desperate.

"Ooma, ooma," sirened Naz, as if I'd injured his inmost id, "what a disappointment you are to me. You, the shining star of Four BEE's Jang, and in such a becoming body."

"Listen," I said, "I know our teeth are reinforced, but unless you shut up, I'm definitely willing to try and knock yours right down your throat."

I got the monitor beam going, but the computer took a while in coming on.

"There's been a mistake," I informed it. "Five Jang have arrived here that didn't mean to—a bird-plane malfunction. Can you send someone to take them back? I don't think they'll make it on their own."

The computer rattled, then:

"Once they have made contact with you, they are to be considered as exiles."

Its metallic voice-tape sounded altered somehow, even less approachable than before.

"God!" I shouted at it, to see what would happen.

"God is a primitive and untenable invention," it promptly replied. Somebody had reprogrammed it. No longer was it a fascinated adversary, it was a cold, cold enemy who wouldn't play games. From here on, its answer would, in every sense, be no.

"OK," I said, "you're being unfair and clunk-headed, but I expected nothing else. Go fry in your storage batteries."

It never even twitched.

Thus, what? Here was I stranded with five awfuls, who would ruin my dream by sheer lack of personality. Yet they *were* outcast. And if I slew them (murderer, killer, why else were you cast from home and dome?) it was PD for them. And maybe even *their* barren little egos were dear to them.

If only Kam were here, Kam and Danor.

But they weren't, and wouldn't be till sunset at the earliest, and I had no means to signal them. I must cope solo.

There was a slender chance.

I went back into the saloon, where Naz lay stretched in midair on a float-cushion he'd got one of the robots to blow up for him.

"Changed your *derisann* mind, *ooma-kasma?*"

"Naz," I said, "I think we ought to talk. I can tell you're

the mainstay of your circle. The others look up to you, don't they? It was your decision to leave the city?"

I'd hit the target, fair and square. He smiled indulgently. Ecstasy had presumably faded from him a little, since he actually heard some of what I said.

"You know, *ooma-kasma*, you know. Well, they've got to have someone. I'm stronger—you think so?—then Phy—he's the other predom male. Loxi's just everywhere and on the moons. Nilla's a girl, never anything but. Ultra-female, you know? Scratchy. Felain, she's predom tangled-up. She sui-cided every day for a whole vrek, got so bad even the Q-Rs thought she'd done it mistakenly. Then they stuffed her in cold store for thirty units. Now she really only wants to go with Nilla, and Nilla won't be a male, and Felain doesn't want to be a male, and it's a real live *floop*-show, *ooma*."

I sat down. As he'd let all this out, a little streak of intelli-gent, bewildered compassion had shown on his face.

"It sounds bad," I said.

"Oh, yes," he said. "Did I tell you Loxi starved himself to death in BAA? Took ninety units. And Phy gets melan-cholia in the dark. When it's night, he'll cry."

"That will be something to look forward to," I said; but my heart was rending me with its claws.

"As for me," he said, "I don't have problems. Life is just one gray-rose nebula from dawn to *grakking* dawn."

And before I could stop him, he'd shoveled handfuls of ecstasy down his throat and was soon floating in every direc-tion, singing: "Oh, it's great, *ooma-kasma*. The ceiling is full of little chandeliers—one, two, three, one, two, three ..."

After this, any attempt to get through to him was a point-less exercise. It was only as I'd caught him on the down-surge of ecstasy that I'd got such a wild repercussion to my mild, would-be clever query.

But I could see their whole circle was in a right mess; not model citizens, just the normal kind, jollity and delight for the skin, neurasthenia in the joints.

Makerish again? *Five* child-substitutes?

Along the corridor, outside the apartments, shouts.

Beyond the closed yellow door, a groaning male voice en-treating: "Nilla, Nilla, do it again." By the closed yellow door, pineapple-curled Felain clenching her fists and yelling, and Loxi saying: "Oh, er, look, *ooma*, for my sake—"

Now ecstasy was wearing thin, their true human traits were showing, their foibles, bad nerves, and wretchedness. Felain was poorly insulated electric fire, Loxi, unideal partner, a tepid, nonquenching puddle.

I put back on the storm I'd lost with Naz.

"You two," I raged, "if you want to live on my land and in my ship, you can just get used to taking orders from me."

"Squiggle off," said Felain, so I spun her around with one hand and smacked her in her delicate puss. I don't like hitting people. They may hit you back. Besides, I didn't want to damage her looks when she was now stuck with this body, and the healing salve was the sum total of what we had till a robot-rescue arrived to set her nose, or whatever.

A welt appeared on her damascene cheek, and having noted she wasn't going to biff me, I felt shame ooze in my spine. But too late for shame, and it wasn't too bad; would pale to nothing in half an hour.

"Now listen, and take this in. You poured off your plane, you trampled through the bushes, you picked the leaves and the flowers. So now you're going to come with me and do some chores out there to make up for the damage. You, Loxi, minus your chains and bells, and you, Felain, in something the briars won't rip off your back in three splits."

Felain lowered her lashes and gave me an unmistakable look through them, so for a moment I felt I was almost back in my male poet's body.

"Yes, *ooma*," she said demurely.

"So. See to your clothes and get outside," I gruffly added, resenting the muddle she was making of my hormones. Loxi flew to obey, and Felain slunk, provocatively.

Within, cries and moans reached a crescendo and dwindled.

"You two," I said through the door, "are to be out on the veranda in twelve splits, dressed for hard work."

"You're kidding," muttered Phy. "I've worked hard enough."

But the crawler's whine was in his voice.

Nilla, the dusky-pink delicacy, who obviously dominated both Phy and Felain, called sweetly:

"Twelve splits is too soon, *ooma-kasma*. Come in and we'll show you why."

So I opened the door and went in, demonstrating that I wasn't to be intimidated.

Quite instructive it was, too, to one of my relatively modest tastes.

"Very artistic," I said, "but you can still make the deadline. If you don't, my robots, which I have programmed to take instructions only from me, will come and bring you out as you are, accessories and all."

I hadn't actually reprogrammed the robots and, having masterfully stridden forth, I rushed to do so. I put in an override order, too, in case anyone tried to block *my* block. Yay, Bross, and Jaska bore it with softly ticking forbearance.

After twenty-five splits. Felainnillaloxiandphy stood uneasily giggling and jostling in the porch, Naz having ecstasied into unconsciousness in the saloon.

I was going to have to teach them to garden, since there was nothing else I could do with them. At least they jumped when I spoke. Even Nilla was being cautious.

Felain sidled by, but I'd calmed myself. Poet no longer. Confront the facts, as a female, it was Hergal I wanted, wormwood truth I would now admit. Never mind. I'd got the upper hand with this lot, for a while anyhow.

And in about two hours the sun would set, and my friends would be coming home to save me from complete collapse.

5

The sun dropped like a jewel below the western horizon. There the mountains seem to sink back into the sands, leaving open that way to the cities from which, half crazy and running, I had come. A western horizon of tall dunes mounted on low rock, taller dunes since the sandstorm, maybe bare stone after the next.

Amber afterglow. Jang strewn along the veranda wailing about bones torn from sockets, muscles liquidized, sunburn. Luckily their skins—not one seemed to have designed a really desert-suited body—had not reacted too badly. Nilla, least burned of everyone, mewed that she was the worst burned. Felain rubbed salve into her, dreamily.

They'd worked very hard. Too hard for themselves, harder than they'd meant to.

Only Nilla still picked flowers. I'd seen her. Just like a child from hypno-school nicking a goody from under a Q-R's nose. Nilla might be a handicap. I was fairly sure she'd done this predominantly female thing only in order to throw her circle off balance, in particular hapless Felain. Still, they were stuck with Nilla as a girl now, Nilla included.

Even Naz had loitered out onto the veranda. He lay on the pillowy couch, humming.

I'd had to warn them not to stare at the sun.

And now the sun had sunk.

I'd been so sure Danor and Kam would be back at this time that I'd been listening and looking around for several splits for their plane. Once I thought I heard it, but was mistaken. I'd been banking on their help in dealing with this mob, most of whom, I had the feeling, hadn't been Jang for very long. Danor was about my age in Janghood, Kam, of course, older.

But the plane didn't come. And didn't come.

The sky emptied out into palest indigo. Stars burned through. The Jang, forgetting to grumble, stared at these

118

phenomena silently, not taking ecstasy or howling about "This is where it's at, *ooma-kasma*," or anything. Even Naz was filling his drug-shadowed eyes.

"There's no moon," complained Nilla.

"So go up and make one," Phy told her. He wasn't crying with melancholia either. If he ever had.

Presently it was a mealtime, and they vaguely went off to eat it, like good children. I'd told them, attempting to intimidate them with numbers, that Danor and Kam would be here later, but they'd forgotten.

I stayed outside, watching, waiting.

They sky darkened. There was a silken rustle of subsiding sand about a mile away, the sound of it trickling easily across those spaces of quiet. The day had tired me out.

The Sisters woke me, punctual as ever. They woke the Jang, too, who had collapsed in comas of exhaustion in the saloon. They came hopping out to see the volcanic fireworks, half-scared, half-admiring.

"Your friends are late," said Naz. "Got any ecstasy? I took all mine and the machines won't dispense; say you programmed the robots to program them not to."

"That's it," I said. "You can forego the ecstasy, or you'll be unfit for work tomorrow."

Naz, lethargically cursing me, meandered off.

No Danor, no Kam.

My guts had turned cold. Irrational. Anything could have delayed them. Most probably trouble with the newly set monitor computer. And yet, and yet.

"Ooh-weeh!" screeched Nilla at the Sisters, more or less in my ear.

I got up. I was going to check with the blasted computer, even if it did mean giving the water-mixer game away.

"I'm inquiring about some fellow exiles of mine," I said. "Danor, female body from BEE, Kam, older male, BAA. They've put down over the mountains from me, eastward, I'm not precisely sure where. Have they been in contact with you on their monitor beam?"

Rattle. (Even the rattle sounded more efficient, more resolute.)

"They have."

"When?"

Click.

"Computed time of desert noon."

"Noon?"

"Noon."

"I wasn't obviously going to get anything for free, so I sold us out.

"What did they want?"

"Two water mixers."

"Oh—ah—how odd!" I, falsely amazed.

"The request was refused," said the computer. "Their plane was given your coordinates and they were told to join you and share your water mixer."

"Did they argue?"

"For approximately one hour."

Good for Kam. I could imagine.

"Didn't work, though, did it?"

"It did not," said the computer, without even a metallic hint of satisfaction.

Heavy chill dark was thick around me, not entirely due to the night beyond the windows.

"So, if they were coming here, I could expect them pretty soon."

Click, click. No answer.

"Well, shouldn't I? Or earlier? About seven hours ago, in fact."

"Unless they have decided to abide by Committee suggestion and order a home built where they are presently located, without growing things."

"Don't try and fool me. You know and I know it was a plot to get a water mixer for us here in the valley. And you know they should be back here now. Did they link with you again?"

"No." Rattle, rattle. "Perhaps they have realized the enormity of what they have done, and elected for suicide and Personality Dissolution."

A white wave broke over me. I cut out the beam link, and stood, holding my breath with tension. Suicide? Not them. So what had happened?

There was a noise on the veranda, shouts, exciting thumpings. The Jang had apparently spotted something. Could it be the plane?

I sped veranda-wards, and emerged among an applauding, pointing mêlée of Felainnillaloxiandphy. Something had come over the eastern mountains and plummeted into the greenery about ten feet from the porch.

"Oh, look, it's a desert bird," they were inanely squawking.

"Out of the way, *floops,* it's an android, and I know it."

It was Danor's swan.

I knelt by the swan, which, exhausted but apparently whole, was recovering in the grass.

"Oh God, swan, what's happened?"

And the swan fluted: "You are the wonderful sun of my sky!" which sent the Jang morons into raptures. But not me. It was the warning song, the song which pleaded for aid.

When they saw my face, the Jang row ebbed.

"Naz," I said, noting him full length on the pillowy couch.

"Sure, I'm awake," said Naz. "Are you going to give me some ecstasy, *ooma,* my *ooma,* or your own nut-brown self?"

"Naz," I said, "I think you've lived longer than the rest of your circle, and I think under your sprawling hide there lurks a spark of intelligence. You and your crowd foisted yourselves on me and I'm stuck with you and you're stuck with me. Just over those mountains there, those low ones, a couple of friends of mine are in trouble. I don't know what kind, but it must be bad. And their monitor beam is probably out so they can't call for city help, all they can hope for is me. Now, listen. I'm going to take Yay—the robot—and your bird-plane, and I'm going over east to look for my friends. While I'm gone, Naz, you'll have charge of your circle. And if I come back and find you've ruined my ship or my Garden, I'll tear you limb from limb and stuff the bits down a sandhole. Is that clear?"

"I'm not clear quite how you'd manage it," drawled Naz.

"I don't think you're entitled to our bird-plane," said Nilla.

"Entitled!" I squalled. "When you think you're entitled to my home and my land and to pick my bloody plants to bloody pieces. Every moment I waste on you, two people out there may be in agony, or *dead* without benefit of Limbo."

That sobered them. Nilla looked down. Naz said:

"Go on then. I'll take charge. How about some ecstasy before you go?"

But I was running, Yay clacketing on my heels, for the plane in the grove of purple trees, so no doubt he didn't catch my obscene answer.

Yay took forever at the controls before we lifted. I'd told him to check them out, remembering the wild Jang landing, and sure enough there was something wrong that he had to correct before we could get airborne.

We made it eventually, up into a black-marble sky veined with faint cloud.

I didn't know exactly where Kam had aimed for—it had been pot-luck, anywhere over the ridge, just so a few miles and rocks stood between their place and mine.

I know that I was thinking even then that they'd crashed, and it seemed so illogical for a plane to malfunction that the computer's words came back and back to me. Maybe the desert had suddenly swelled up around them, huge and terrifying, a delayed phobia, robbing them of courage, sense, even of love. Maybe suicide, or panic, had caused Kam's blue plane to dive into oblivion. But no, I couldn't believe it. Wouldn't.

There were a good four hours of darkness left as we searched along the eastern ridges, scouring them with the plane's underlights. Twice we went over the Cup, and I could look down past its rim into a vast, extinct volcanic crater; truly it was a cup, even inside, and once that bowl had brimmed with fire.

Near dawn we landed to recharge the friction batteries, which were crackling fretfully, then, after half an hour, went up again.

First pallid intimations of sun-arrival on the sky far below.

With daylight, it should be easy to spot . . . anything, not of the desert.

I saw the wreckage one hour after sunrise.

It lay along a sandy shelf, smoking dustily. Shadow and night had hidden it, for we'd passed this area before. From the positioning they'd been on their way back to the sandship, coming from the dunes beyond the eastern mountain slopes.

I shut my eyes and each of my senses when I saw. I felt no grief, no sickness, and no anger, only a great blank of nothing.

But I made Yay land our plane. I had to be certain they were dead, and then I had to get back and contact Limbo. Ego-death was better than absolute death, and so we all believed. Dangor and Kam would be Danor and Kam no longer, but, *rorls* in the future, they'd come back from PD at least living.

I wasn't relishing the thought of what I'd find—stray

human parts, blood . . . The plane made a perfect touch-down on the rocks. I opened up and got out.

Then I heard the new noise, the thrub-thrub of motors in the sky I had just vacated.

I stared up. A tiny black dot circling westward. Limbo—it looked like Limbo even from this distance. Limbo robots zooming in to save the life sparks of Danor and Kam.

Yes, circling nearer, I could see now it was a Limbo craft. Circling nearer, near enough to check, with its beamers, life or death below; circling, but not landing. Not *landing*. Then—

I looked again, past the wreck to where the rock shelved up into a hollow arching, hiding its cavelike depth from the sky above. And I saw Danor standing there gazing back at me, and Kam about a yard in front of her.

I ran, and they ran, panting in the thin air. The three of us ran together and more or less collided. We clung to each other on the rock, muttering things that made no sense, and overhead the dark city messenger droned away.

"They've only got Joyousness laid on in their stupid Jang plane," I said, "but if you don't mind a bit of ecstasy, it's not bad."

"After yesterday," said Kam, "ecstasy would be a pleasant change."

So we drank Joyousness and ate toasted angelfood, which was the only thing their first-meal-dispenser button would give us (typical).

And then a tale was unfolded. Kam's account and Danor's. I'd like to write it in the old way, with ink and pen, frame it in gold, and set it up in the ship's saloon for everyone to see.

Having asked Four BEE for the water mixer, argued, and got nowhere, they set the controls for my ship and up they went. Presently there came a clucking in the panel. Kam checked and got the panel to check itself. The panel told him it had malfunctioned, and it was too late to right itself since something had snapped somewhere and poured off oil into the batteries. About two splits later the batteries cut out.

Danor said she stood there, wan and useless, just expect-ing to take his hand and say goodbye. But Kam pulled all the guts from the float-bed and they baled out on them. It was brilliant and chancy, but it was the only chance they had. Luck and the float-gas held, and they escaped with minor abrasions, falling on the rocks about fifty feet below the spot where the plane itself crashed, and slowly climbing up to it, no easy task without oxygen tablets.

The monitor beam had had it, but they reasoned that this fault would duly have registered in Four BEE, and a rescue plane would come to see what sort of situation they were in, salve their cuts, and probably dump them back in my valley.

Around sunset they heard the throb of motors, left the overhang where they'd sheltered from the sun, and waved clothing and arms about. Sure enough the plane came closer and closer. Soon it was close enough to see it was a Limbo item. Certainly it saw them. In the gathering gloom they made out the flash of its beams, registering them.

But it didn't land. Just circled there. After about ten splits it went away.

It gets cold in the desert at night, particularly up in the mountains; the stars hammer on the rock and strike frost. Kam raided the plane wreck, and managed to coerce some warmth out of a dying battery or two. It got them through the night, with no margin.

Just before dawn the Limbo plane came over again. It's a wonder I didn't bang right into it, but I and it must have sidled by each other in the darkness somewhere, and the sound of my own motors camouflaged it. It circled them once more and went away. They knew by then.

There used to be a certain bird in the desert, but I think it is extinct by now. It lived off carrion and, noting a dying animal from on high, it would circle there, watching, till the last spark of life went out. Then swoop and devour the corpse.

The plane from Limbo had been watching. It was waiting for Kam and Danor to die. They had a vast choice of deaths. The natural ones of exposure—too much sun, or too much cold—or starvation, dehydration, or oxygen deficiency. Or they could hurl themselves from the rocks, or find a handy bit of metal in the wreck and slash a vein. Once dead, the Limbo plane would swoop and carry them safe to PD in the city.

I suppose with me, the first exile, the one the Committee had outcast themselves, they'd felt obliged to observe the rules. But with voluntary exiles, PD was obviously the best place for them, and the quicker they got there the better. So the Committee was kind enough to help them make their decision.

It was horrifying. It was true fear with a naked face.

Could they still, those compassionate Q-Rs programmed so long ago to serve humankind, be kidding themselves that they were acting in humanity's best interests, protecting us from ourselves? Or had the old grievance at last asserted itself, the grievance that twelve *vreks* before had suggested itself to my instincts? Even in the tanks, you can't breed a human without the relevant cells from two other humans; however, given these cells, the child comes alive and grown on its own. But the Q-R, bred from selected metals and flesh—man outside, machine inside—is born from a blueprint on the great farm at BAA, and brought to life by the force of an electronic charge. They have no actual life *spark*, no "soul" as the ancients termed it. Could it be that they'd come to resent the lack? Or had the blueprint itself somewhere gone wrong?

When they bailed out, Kam had taken the swan, but the floater wouldn't tolerate the combined weight or the swan's kicking, so he had to push it off, trusting to the memory that it had flown before—one of the few things it could do. And, after dropping like a stone for a couple of feet, the swan opened its wings and saved itself very efficiently. Once they were all down, the swan had stamped about the terrain discontentedly, obviously under the impression that Danor had organized the crash on purpose, for some incomprehensible reason. Finally it vanished, and neither of them could find it. In the circumstances, confronted with doom as they were, they thought it possibly for the best that the swan had deserted them. Perhaps it would make out in the desert, even get back to the valley. They had considered that possibility, too, but, inadequately clothed, with no oxygen or water, they wouldn't have lasted an hour on those treacherous slopes.

Danor was bowled over by the swan's display of concern and intelligence on reaching me. I mentioned the Jang only briefly. It would be bad enough to have them in our laps on our return, and we had no dearth of problems.

The oxygen pump in the Jang plane was doing wonders for Kam and Danor. So were the Joyousness and angelfood, surprisingly enough. They were both tanned almost black, of course, but otherwise seemed OK. Only their eyes retained the darkness, the knowledge of that fate the Committee had intended for them. Beyond the bare facts, we hadn't spoken of it too much.

At length I tapped Yay, and the plane, overcrowded again, lifted up into the sky and headed homeward.

It was a beautiful morning.

6

The moment we were in sight of the valley, I could tell there was trouble. Don't know why, unless it was that thick black column of smoke wending up into the ether.

My first thought was that the Jang had razed my sand-ship to the ground and half the Garden with it.

But then I made out that the smoke arose from a point just beyond the western perimeter of the Garden, and my plot and home were untouched.

We landed in the grove of purple trees—why not? The grass had been flattened by the first arrival, and Yay, more careful than the Jang, did no further damage to the boughs. I got out first and at once they were on me—Nillaloxiandphy.

"*Ooma, ooma,*" they bellowed. "Three more, three more fellow exiles!"

"*Derisann,*" I said. They hadn't bothered to ask if my friends were found, safe or dead.

Nilla added:

"That swan thing pecked me." Never a cloud without a silver lining.

Naz came strolling up. He lounged against a tree.

"Like it's all happening," said Naz. "Did you see the smoke? Their plane went out of control, but they got clear before it blew up. And guess what, *ooma-kasma,* they're Older People. Did you get your circle together over the mountains?"

"Yes, thanks. But Kam and Danor aren't my circle. Circles ceased to exist the moment you left the city. Where are these three arrivals?"

They were on the veranda, sipping Joyousness quite unworriedly.

A male, two females. They all had garnet hair, attractive, healthy tan bodies, and smiles. I had time to notice Felain seated by one of the women, looking fascinated and fascinating, the swan comfortably asleep in her lap, when the

127

male jumped up, advanced on me, and grabbed me in a sort of passionately platonic embrace.

"My dear!" he cried. "We are overwhelmed by your achievements. We have been saying for two *rorls* that the young have the perfect kind of uncluttered, headstrong wilfulness that was needed to give the Fours a smart kick in the pants. I hope you'll forgive our intrusion. We aren't planning to live on your doorstep, so to speak, but near at hand, if you'll permit."

"They won't give you a water mixer," I found myself saying.

I was confused and overtired, and these three looked so alike.

"Then we'll build our own," said the older male.

"Your own what?"

"Water mixer, my dear. I have wasted several very boring *vreks* among the army of Committee-employed Older Persons, bungling about with a lot of buttons that would go off on their own anyway, but it has taught me, unintentionally, the odd bit of mechanical knowhow. I see you laugh, and rightly so. What is this silly old fool rambling on about? Good for you. Never respect years, only deeds."

"But I wasn't laughing at you. It's just that I've seen a few Older Persons employed, and I agree, but I never realized they realized—" I stopped, having tied myself in a knot, but he got the gist. His eyes were awfully bright and rather mad, but he looked—refreshing somehow. The left-hand female was stroking Felain's pineapple hair with a gentle open friendly sensuality that surprised and encouraged my liking.

"Ah, yes," said the mad male, "let me but explain. We three were part of a great Jang circle in our youth, a *rorl* back. We're very ancient, you see, and never had PD. As older people we have fermented rather than matured. We hung out in BAA, but this looks much more like it. We've often tripped off into the desert for mid-*vrek*. Ever met that idiot Assule—calls himself a *Glar?* Good, good. Then you'll know what a pest he is. Spent eighty units with him on some ruin he'd dug up, and him pissing himself at the idea of grubbing about in the dirt instead of a robot. Got a whole vase out myself, with my bare hands. Had a picture of a galloping ponka herd painted round the sides. Till the damned bugger came creeping up and screamed in my ear: 'Ah! You *touched* it!' Dropped the bloody thing, of course."

I nearly laughed myself sick. The mad male looked gratified.

"I'm Moddik," he said. "The ladies are Talsi, and Glis with the pretty pineapple girl. Now, about this water mixer—"

"Wait, wait," I cried. Everything was going too fast. "My two friends back there have been stranded on a mountain all night, and I'm nearly off my feet. Would you forgive us if we called it quits till this evening? I think we ought to have some sort of meeting, all of us, to try to sort everything out. We'll need to pool our knowledge and so on, and I'm too woolly-headed right now."

'Nonsense," said Moddik, "I don't believe it. However, we'll be quite perfect till later, exploring the potential of your splendid valley. Did you know you have *binnimasts?*"

Nervously I glanced at myself, thinking I'd broken out into some rare skin disease.

"Er, no . . ."

"Yes, you do. A whole colony of them. Look, there's one now!"

I turned and saw a lemon object rolling in the sunlight.

"Oh, they're *binnimasts*, are they? I called them Gray-Eyeses."

"Did you? Much better too. *Graks* to *binnimasts*. Gray-Eyeses it is."

7

I sank into sleep and dreamed of Moddik the mad male with a long white beard, and looking quite ancient though very sprightly, for his young body had been well and truly belied by his tones. He was jumping about over the archaeological site with an inexhaustible supply of pitchers of sapphire wine, one of which, every so often, he would drop with a thudding crash. From a nearby pillar hung the flayed skin of *Glar* Assule, a fact which filled me with delight rather than apprehension. Elevated on a cloud sat a Q-R Committee. They aimed lightning bolts at Moddik, which he effortlessly dodged. Where they hit the ground, they turned into the wreckage of bird-planes, and out of each lot of wreckage emerged beautiful joyful people, laughing. "You won't get us that way, you steel-arsed bastards," warbled Moddik. And apparently they didn't.

Danor woke me, gently, just before sunset.

She had a rough message to make up for it.

The Nillaloxiandphy brigade had the Picture-Vision on, and there had been a flash broadcast—just like when they flashed out the film of Me in the Waste. I'd missed it, being asleep, but Kam, hearing the row the others made, went in and caught the end. Moddik and Talsi were out in the Garden, Glis and Felain in one of the cabins, apparently, and didn't respond, so they missed it too.

Once so rare, flash interruptions to Picture-Vision seemed on the increase indeed. Neither were they normally relayed out-dome. It rather looked as though the Committee had made sure we got this one on our wall, in addition to the citizens of Four BEE. And they said they were going to repeat the flash. The hour they gave corresponded chronologically to desert sunset.

I flew about, demented, and grabbed the nearest article of clothing, which turned out to be my party outfit, meant for yesterday, Looking incongruously glamorous in amber with amethyst scintilla, and a nervy frown, I arrived in the P-V room just in time. Not a large area, it was now packed with the Jang and the three older outcasts. Danor's swan had sat in a seat and wouldn't be moved—it had pecked Nilla again when she tried. Danor and I perched by the wall with Kam.

Presently the flowery orgies faded off the screen, and a solemn Q-R appeared. The Jang promptly made crude noises and shushed each other. The Q-R produced a second or so of guff about not alarming anybody, and how unhappy he—the Q-R—was about the situation and the action that had to be taken. Then he gave a brief résumé of the events which led up to my exiling—accurate, I had to admit, if biased—my departure, and the film they'd shown of me. Several misguided citizens had since followed me. Of course, they were the lunatic fringe, and perhaps safer in exile. However, the valley was now a hotbed of unbalanced, anti-city activity. In order to discourage further of these misguided citizens from leaving the dome in order to join the misanthropic band, the Committee wished it to be known that in the future, aid and supplies to the exiles would be limited to the barest minimum. They could expect oxygen, vitamins, the basics of food materials, but no luxuries (a kind of protein porridge would be all we'd be able to coax from the provision dispenser, once our current supply of syntho ran out, and no drinks, ecstasy, energy, or similar). Water mixers we had, and must make them go around, rationing in emergency, but we might ask for painkilling drugs and medicinal salve should we require them. Anything more drastic and we could forget it. (Thank God, I thought, thank God Danor and Kam hadn't sustained serious injury.) Building materials would be sent to us on request, but in specific form, nothing left for us to shape to our own ends. In fact we'd get nothing at all they thought we might be dangerously creative with. We were on our own. And we were to be left on our own. No one else was going to join us. No sand-ships, bird-planes, or other vehicles would be given to those known to be sympathetic to us. Those with their own planes would have their licenses withdrawn. Private flights outside the domes were prohibited forthwith and until further notice, and general intercity traffic would be restricted. Citizens were asked to bear with us this inconvenience in the interest of communal harmony.

Lastly, the Q-R said, staring out at us from the wall, his face without malice or pretension, only sad—self-convinced, at least— "The unhealthy craze which has swept the cities will shortly evaporate. The exiles will be left to their own devices. Having defied order and the laws of order, they can hardly expect the Committee to keep them in dome-fashion, free of charge. Their plight is sorry and pathetic, and will presently be resolved in mutual suicide and PD, which is still open to them, and will always be open to them until they are ready to return to it."

The image faced, and roses fell down the wall. The flash was over. We switched off and sat in silence. Then Kam said quietly:

"They added a line or two this time. And they were using upper-tonal to emit a depressing atmosphere."

I hadn't got that, and was relieved, for depression had swamped me and I'd thought it was me. The Jang, obviously relieved too, booed and blared militantly.

Suddenly Moddik was on his feet.

"Load of rubbish," he said vehemently. "Silly nonhuman fools." He shot a glance at me. "You look as if you agree. Splendid. Just give their basic food elements to me when they come in, and I'll fiddle about with them a bit. The meals ought to be even better than they are now. Besides which, half the stuff can simply be reprogrammed from its own leftovers. All you need is an infinitesimal atom of fire-apple and you can process for fire-apple till the sun falls. Food machines don't need great shovelsful of the muck to do an analysis. Our precious androids are just trying to flummox us and everyone else, and it won't work. As for their building specifics, I'd like to see them foist a prefabricated utility-palace off on *me*. And I know a way to get a blueprint for water mixers and just about everything else, simply by wiring one of your robots into the original model for a couple of hours."

We gawped at him with mingled hope and disbelief.

"Come on. Get your jaws off the mosaic," he said. And to me: "Where's the meeting you spoke of earlier, and when?"

"The saloon," I said. "Now."

Not a very orderly meeting.

First of all, Loxi fingering the fringe on my dress and "Oh, *ooma*, I had one like this once, when I was a girl—in BAA— all flames it was . . ." Naz moaning about ecstasy, and Phy suddenly breaking down in floods of tears, his darkness-melancholia finally catching up, or just plain fear at our plight. Talsi, the non-Felain-fancying older woman, comforted him in a makerish—no, be precise—*maternal* way, very touching to behold. Danor and Kam sat close to each other, calm as could be, secure in their bond. I didn't feel jealous any more, but a sort of hollow place had come in my heart, and notices stood on the bare sand of it which read: "Vacant, and never now to be filled."

"Very well," I said, when things had settled a little, "we each know adequately who everyone is, and what our own and each other's problems are likely to be, so maybe we don't need to go into that right at this split. Our total numbers are eleven, not enormous, and our sexual leanings, despite our current bodies, seem fairly fluid, so I'm not sticking any labels on anyone. We're going to have to cope with that as best we can, since we probably won't have a chance of changing for the rest of our lives." The slight murmuring that had started up fell off again at this doomful clarion call. "However," I tritely said, "situations have a habit of altering unexpectedly. Who knows what tomorrow may bring.?"

"Sand fleas?" volunteered Nilla.

"From here on," I said pointedly, "we have to work together where possible, and try not to drive each other *zara-dann*. For this purpose I suggest splitting up, and not living altogether in a bunch here on the ship. If Moddik can do what he says in the way of adapting—"

"I can do more than I say," interposed Moddik flatly.

"Yah, yah," said Naz. "Has yet to be seen, my *soolka* old *ooma*."

"Good," said Moddik. "Healthy opposition. I may clip you around the chops, young man, but don't let that stop you. How many water mixers were you wanting?" His bright glance flashed at me like a couple of steel animals up on their hind legs, ready for havoc.

"About nine," I said, to gauge his reaction. "But that's for the valley. We'll need more for the extra homes if we're going to have them."

Moddik nodded, got up, and went out.

I thought we'd offended him or something, but Glis smiled at me and said:

"He really is entirely brilliant. He's going to wire up your third robot—Borss, is it?—for the blueprint to the water-mixer outside. He'll also use the monitor beam to request building materials. When they arrive, he'll start reconstructing. You simply have to understand the principle of reprocessing, and then you can alter any substance eventually to fit your needs."

"And Moddik does," I said.

"Oh, yes."

"It sounds impossible to me."

"Oh, no. After all, most of the machines can do it, and once you grasp the fundamentals of the mechanical brain, which Moddik has, it's easy."

"Oh yes?"

"When we were at hypno-school, two *rorls* back," put in Talsi, rocking the now smiling Phy upon her walnut satin bosom, "they sometimes gave awards for signs of genius. In those units it was even possible to make some sort of career for yourself if you wished to and were clever enough. Moddik won all the awards. Glis was a little boy when she was a child, and also very talented. I'm the stupid one. But I have a strong makerish streak, as you see, tied into my sex drive, so I shall be quite useful." She beamed about, managing to catch Naz' eye, Loxi's eye, and even mine. Phy's she didn't need to catch.

Right then Moddik strode back in, and he'd done as Glis had said.

"I'm very glad you got through to the computer," I said. "I wasn't sure the link would still operate." And with only this for introduction, I told them what had happened to Kam and Danor, after which Kam and Danor were madly questioned by hysterical Jang and briefly and sanely questioned by mad Moddik. Having established the facts to everyone's horror, I thought I'd better add the final grim epilogue—or prologue? "Something has gradually become clear to me, one rather gruesome truth. Which is that, of all the three birdplanes that came out here, not one was without a malfunction. Moddik, Glis, and Talsi's plane was out of control on landing and went up like a rocket just after. Danor and Kam's plane got here OK, but on the second flight spilled oil into the batteries and nosedived. The Jang plane made a rotten touchdown so I got my robot Yay to check and correct it, and if I hadn't I imagine my body would now be tastefully bedecking the mountains in various stages of incompleteness. This coincidence seems rather odd, to me. Even my sand-ship wasn't of the best, and the provision dispenser exploded at the first possible opportunity." There was silence thick as velvet in the saloon. You could hear the desert night wind furling round the ship. "How often do planes malfunction in the city? Ever? Perhaps once every *rorl*. Now, I'm not saying the Committee has done anything positive, but I do think that maybe they've let their robots get deliberately careless, forgotten to service the servicing machines, something like that. I don't quite know how they managed, since they're supposed to be permanently programmed to protect human life. Possibly they've got around it by re-collecting that even when we die we don't actually *die*, and what's mere Ego-Death to an android? Our life spark goes on, they see to that. I don't know. My theories are embryonic and the whole thing scares me. But I know this. By one means or another, subtly, unconsciously even, they are out to get us. They want the desert clear of us and our anti-city-system ideas. They fear that we'll overthrow the harmonic rule of law and order, bring civil collapse, anarchy, and destruction in our wake—God knows how, but that's the core of the matter. So we'd better watch out from here on. Every supply the city sends us we'll machine-check, just in case someone's omitted something and the next prefabricated building block goes into automatic combustion and blows us all to PD." I paused, about long enough to take a breath. "I might add that food has been growing here on the northwest side, and the toxicity check has proved negative. For my eighth meal tonight I'm going to sample home-grown produce. If it's pleasing, we can extend the venture. Self-sufficiency isn't a bad thing to aim for, particularly placed as we are."

Everybody stared at me. Even the shock of Q-R treachery had been slightly muffled by surprise at the food announcement.

"*I'm* not eating it," said Nilla predictably. "I bet it's absolutely *drumdiky*."

"No one's asking you to," I said. "I've explained that I'll do it."

"Splendid heroic attitude," said Moddik. "It's probably delicious. But one point. The city syntho-food contains certain additives. Introduce additive-free substances into yourself and your body chemistry may change."

"Yes, I realize that," I said, "but I think I'll acclimatize. If I don't, no one else will try, that's all."

Felain and Loxi were looking at me worshipfully. Danor looked faintly troubled. Kam said:

"I'd like to volunteer to do it myself. You're the founder of this enterprise. It shouldn't fall to you."

"It's the very reason why it *should*," I said.

I felt quite glad of their admiration or concern. Actually I had total faith in my ability to survive a few rosy fruits and a slice or so of tuber, or I'd never have done it. After all, it was city food to begin with, if unmixed and now intermingled with the properties of the wild. Somehow, having gone through so many traumas with the desert and survived, I'd come to feel there was nothing further to fear from it. An adversary to respect, to battle with, but not a mean one, not underhand. If it came at you, it came head-on, with a storm or an eruption or a tribe of marauding ski-feet. Not slyly, with a juicy fruit whose pips, germinating in some inner tract, would turn my skin green and scaly or my voice into a bark. Besides which, the negative tests showed that any effects that did crop up would be minor and easily reversed.

You don't get a coward like me being a heroine with a *real* dragon about. I hang my sword on the wall, and get under the float-bed, *ooma*.

8

What a night.

No one went to sleep. I think Nilla kept up to see if I'd go into a fit after my eighth meal of grown food. I could just visualize her standing interestedly over my spasming wracked body, saying: "How frantically *drumdik, ooma-kasma*. What a *floopy* thing."

Actually, the only symptom the food produced in me was a desire for more. It was marvelous—fruits like nectar, tubers tart and succulent. The assembled company watched me eating, and followed me uneasily about afterward, patently expecting me to drop dead, despite the toxicity tests. Even Kam asked a couple of times if I was OK. The two-*rorl* older people were less bothered, and about Sister-blasting time, I caught Moddik in the saloon, nibbling a fruit.

"I thought we agreed," I said.

"Couldn't resist," said Moddik. "We can compare dermatoses later. It's not, my young friend, that I don't entirely defer to your leadership."

"I'm not the leader here," I said, slightly unnerved.

"Are you not? Just wait till the next crisis and we shall all be there, bleating about your feet for directions."

"Then I absolutely abdicate."

"You won't, you know. Like most loners," said Moddik, "you carry the seeds of violent authority. Loners need to be bossy. They quickly learn it's the only method they have of shoving people off their backs."

This conversation stuck in my craw, mainly because it had the doleful ring of logic.

Moddik next informed me, as we gazed from the veranda at the nightly dual eruption in the south, that he'd noticed a few additional edible items growing here and there westward. Somehow he seemed to know what everything was for—sunpeaches, fat green roots, a nut tree which wouldn't bear, he said, for about a *vrek*, and might need extra water, even vines from which we could make our own purely fruit-based wine.

"Moddik," I said, "you've been here before, haven't you? I mean, done something like this?"

He chuckled like a wicked little old man in a book, his young tan face crinkling like the dunes themselves with almost harmless vitriol.

"Not quite. I piddled around somewhat with a hydroponics garden in my youth."

"You're going to be a great asset, Moddik," I said. "Thank goodness you came. Why ever did you?"

"And why did you?" said Moddik.

Not long after he went charging off and came charging triumphantly back with Borss, ghastly with exposed wires and plates unscrewed. Apparently we had the water-mixer blueprint. Presently everybody had to get chemical-fire lamps and follow our magician off to the west, where his plane had exploded, and here, under the whip of his instructions, we poked and probed about in the sand and smoke for bits of scorched metal, plasti-ware, and glacia-view.

"You'd be surprised what use I can put this to," said he.

"*I* shouldn't," spat Nilla.

Moddik roared with laughter, and then he went over and lifted Nilla up in the air, looking strong as a robot and mad as mad. Nilla struggled faintly and seemed scared and pleased.

"So, little predominantly-female-who-isn't, you think the nasty old Moddik gets his thrills that way, do you? I much prefer beating the weak and helpless to a pulp."

Following this exchange, Nilla regarded him with a smoldering resentful interest.

Eventually he herded us back to the ship, and I was astonished to see that Yay and Jaska had put up a sort of shelter place for him over in a clearing near the grove of purple trees. I remembered I'd reset the robots to take orders only from me, but naturally, in Moddik's clever case, this had meant nothing.

"My workshop," said Moddik, and went inside with Borss of the trailing wires. Shortly, a frightening sound of bangs, thuds, and drilling burst upon the fragrant air.

The sun leaped up behind the eastern peaks as I sat alone on the veranda in my now somewhat stained and tattered finery.

The Jang had finally retired in odd order—Felain and Glis, Loxiandphy both with smiling, voluptuous Talsi, Nilla petulantly alone (ha!), Naz euphorically with handfuls of ecstasy Moddik had indulgently conjured for him, after I'd said oh, all right, all right, to his never-ending lament. Danor and Kam, arm in arm, close as leaf on leaf in our Garden, closer than ever since that night on the mountain when death was closer still: close as the world itself. I, who rescued them, had approached the outskirts of their citadel, but no more. How could it be more?

It was a little like one of those ancient plays, which Moddik said were still put on in his youth, when all the characters leave the stage but one. Now for my soliloquy.

Not quite alone, however. The swan, adventurously, had flown up onto the ship's roof and made a nest or something over the cooler vents, which would probably get blocked with its feathers. And from the strange shelter where Moddik still lurked came a pale busy humming.

The water mixer—did it know it had been blueprinted, was no longer unique of its kind?—arose on its tall legs and marched away, tender-pink nozzles spraying.

Sunlight stirred the avenues of the forest to an incredible scalding green. Beyond the Gardens, the desert painted rainbows.

A sort of happy sadness enveloped me. So beautiful, the dawn, and hope like the oxygen bright in the air, and I alone. Yes, the swan was noiseless on the roof, Moddik's shelter humming grew faint as the whispering of the insects waking in the bushes.

Now I should close my eyes. And become the princess on the gate of her silver tower, waiting for her lover to ride, the somber warrior on his starry beast, across the glistening acres of the sand.

I had shut my eyes. Self-disgust made me open them.

And something was sparkling out there. Look down through the forest, beyond the slope of the Garden, way out to the dunes beneath the black upthrust backdrop of the eastern mountains. Something.

But what? No ships or planes would be taking this road, not for many a *vrek*, if ever. A rogue machine on the rampage? But from where?

Maybe there was a simple explanation: e.g., I was going nuts.

"Moddik!" I shouted. "Moddik! Hey! Help!"

He came out into the clearing, his hands full of bolts, rivets, and panes of ice-glass I didn't know we possessed.

"Sorry to break up your genius activities, but would you step up here and tell me if I'm hallucinating?"

He stepped up and looked out. Then, from a bejeweled pouch in his tunic he produced a lens, and looked through that.

"Ah!" said Moddik. "Might have guessed. Can't keep everyone in line, not even in the Fours." He handed me the lens, and I, too, looked through its telescopic sight.

There wasn't an excess of detail, the distance was still too great, but just enough to make me shiver, and glance around to be sure it *wasn't* a silver tower gate I was mooning away on. The figure out there was a dark silhouette in the sun, but male he was, riding on a starry beast. A real starry beast —a dragon of diamonds with eyes of gold, and striding a good twelve feet from the ground on huge prismatic paws.

"I believe it's an android animal from BAA," said Moddik admiringly. "Lad must have stolen it. Enterprising young devil. I guessed that Q-R rubbish wouldn't stop them coming out, not the really determined ones."

My legs were shaking and I wasn't quite certain why, or wouldn't let myself be.

"Thanks, Moddik," I said. "I'd better go and meet him." Moddik grinned and I added lamely: "Before that dragon thing stamps down half the Garden."

9

Even the shadows were green in the Garden. I'd felt tired before; I was wide awake now. Just because I was going out to collect some dope of a Jang male off the dunes, probably tossing ecstasy down his throat, and howling. *"Attlevey, ooma-kasma,* it's *insumattly derisann,* believe me, and I'm all up on the stars, you bet."

Garden's End was still about half a mile off, though the perimeter seemed to be widening itself a little, small dry grasses seeding, pastel-yellow thistle flowers clutching the sand. Coming from the shade, the sun strikes like a blow on the skull. I thought, collecting it for the three-thousandth time, I ought to get the machines to make me one of those old tribal sun-hat things, an *oopsa* or *oosha* or whichever. But I was brooding on down-to-earth practical details in order to stop my fantasies racing up my spine into my brain like an invading horde.

The beast was striding on toward the sand-ship, and me, only a few hundred yards off now over the dunes.

It was almost like a return of my agoraphobia, those few splits I was crossing the open sand. I was half scared to look up, even when the ink-black shadow of the gemstone animal fell thankfully around me. However, shading my eyes with an arm from the elbow of which amethyst trimmings still dripped, I raised my eyes, and stared aloft at the dragon's rider.

"Nice weather," he flippantly remarked. "Bit warm. But nice."

A lot of things hit me at once. I wasn't ready for any of them.

"Who are you?" I demanded, gritting my teeth with a sensation of white-hot lava crowding me from my flesh.

"My name's Esten," he said. *"Derisann* to meet you."

"Damn you, you've got a *farathooming* bloody cheek. What are you up to, you bastard? What's the *grakking* game, you—"

"Esten," he supplied graciously, as if I'd forgotten, and was only filling in with insults to cover the lapse.

"Balls, Esten," I said. "How'd you get it? Where'd you get it? Why'd you come here in it?"

"Oh, *this?* You mean the body, do you?"

"What else, you God-forgotten *floop* of a Jang *thalldrap?*"

"Oh, well," he said, and just waved his hand ever so vaguely, and smiled. It was a long-fingered artistic hand and a charming unexpected smile, the smile of a poet for an attractive girl, the bittersweet greeting of one who is a lover of life despite the tragic death that is slowly, inevitably, devouring him. I knew it pretty well, and not surprising.

He was in my body. The last one, the poet's, slight and graceful build, aquilinity of feature, mane of loosely curling dark hair and large shadow-smudged blue opal eyes and all.

He hadn't missed a trick. Not a *farathooming* one.

Even the gestures were mine.

Only the tan was different, designed to take the sun. Dying of consumption the poet might be, but he didn't fancy sunburn on top of it.

"Well," I said, "I'm waiting."

"And very lovely you look doing it," he said, gallantly. I must have looked, actually, like an electric circuit about to blow its valves out. I tried to calm down.

"Either you tell me," said I, in a measured, steely voice, if a bit heat-melted at the edges, "why you chose to arrive like that, or you can turn your—your whatever-it-is around, and prance off back to BAA."

"I can't do that," he said. "You know it."

"Then explain your conduct. Quickly."

He gave the BAA dragon a little tap and it gracefully knelt. He gracefully slid off and leaned there on its side, immaculately fragile. Oh, I knew that stance. He must have seen the pot boiling over again, because he held up one of those poet-swordfighters's hands and said:

"It's quite simple and perfectly mundane. You'll be sick if I tell you."

"You'll be sicker if you don't."

"Very well, my lady of Jang. I saw the magic film, the film of the enchantress in the waste with her green garden. And I lost mind, soul, and heart. To you."

"Crap," I politely replied.

"Possibly. I told you you'd be nauseated. But you insisted on knowing my reasons, so it's your own fault. There is something about your unique brand of boorish, arrogant stupidity that ties me up in a bow. So adventurous, so cynical, such a funny combination of valor and cowardice, idiocy and intelligence. Your dear little face being all lick-arse to the Committee while obscene signs shone from your eyes like neons. I knew at once I'd never fancy another female as long as I lived. So. I traveled to BAA in the legitimate last public sand-ship running, intrigued my way into the android-animal breeding-tank domes outside the city, persuaded some *floop* of an Older woman to let me try a quick dash over the sandy waste on a dragon, and never bothered to go back."

"What about oxygen?" I said.

"They keep supplies on the out-city farms in case they need to leave the farm-domes in a hurry. Oxygen, anti-dehydration tablets, meal injections, the lot. I nicked what I required when the Older lady was resting, after our little—er—chat."

"Fascinating," I said. "You still haven't mentioned my—your—body."

"Obsessed with you as I was, what else could I do the moment I reached BAA, than order a replicate? It seemed also an excellent way to instant seduction. You've heard the theory, I suppose, that most of us only want to make love to ourselves? Here's your chance, *ooma*. A never-to-be-repeated offer."

He didn't make a move, however, just went on looking at me.

I knew the theory fine. Another thing he'd stolen from me. Something in it, too, if my reactions were anything to go by. My heart was slamming about in my throat, and the other responses—those denied hormones pining so long—were leaping and prancing like things possessed. So, of course, I resented it. His cunning plot, my physical inebriation. And I didn't trust him, he was too clever.

"You're too clever," I said. "I don't trust you. I'm not sure I believe you, either."

"My oxygen ran out last night," he said. "This slightly asthmatic wheeze isn't part of the act, it's real. If I collapse at your feet, will you take me in?"

"Forget it," I said. "One point you overlooked. I know the line; I should, I invented it. Get back on your animal and follow me. I suppose I'm stuck with you the way I'm stuck with all the rest of them."

"Won't you join me on the dragon?"

"No, thanks *awfully*."

So he swung back up, and the beast rose, and they paddled behind me over the last stretch of sand, along the steel paths of the Garden, to the ship.

It wasn't a pleasure to watch him. I think a small part of me was emerald with envy. After all, I'd hopped it from that excellently designed skin before I was really ready. Now, here he was, poetically swooning all over my veranda, with a reemerged Nilla scurrying to bring him food, drink, and cushions, and even Felain and Glis out and about, Glis getting medical machines to take his pulse and Felain cooing in his ears.

I stood at the other end of the veranda and sulked, glaring around with an air of rabid interest in the state of the climbing plants, the sky, the day. When Felain kissed his hand, I got off the veranda and went stalking toward Moddik's workshop.

The dragon had nodded off enormously in the grass at the forest's edge. It was a full android, with no need for food or water. Little curls of scented smoke came from its nostrils. Rather nice it was really, but, unfairly tarred with his brush, I hadn't gone for it much before. What would the Gray-Eyeses (*binnimasts*) think of it? And the swan? That was better, I was cooling down a little.

I knocked on Moddik's weird-shelter door. A strange clattering ensued. Then the door opened to reveal Moddik among a confused undergrowth of wires, steel frames, and transparent webbing. I began to believe what they'd said, he and Glis, about his knowing how to get anything from anything, as a machine does. In Moddik's case, the *rorls* had obviously been put to good use. Everywhere actual machines were clicking and spatting, and Borss had been propped like a demoralized drunk in the corner.

"Is the arrival pleasing?" asked Moddik, tactfully blunt. "Is our young leader glad?"

"No, our young leader isn't glad. The arrival's Jang, and he's had the abysmal gall to turn up here in my last male body—or a replicate."

"Ah!" said Moddik. "I said he was enterprising, did I not? An acquaintance of yours, perhaps, from Four BEE?"

"You know, that never occurred to me. He says his name's Esten, and I never met an Esten that I recall. He doesn't behave like anyone I knew. Or even misbehave like them."

"His manner may be assumed, carefully worked out beforehand in order to mislead. His name could also be false, since, out-dome, it hardly matters."

I sat down to muse on this and hastily got up again with a yell. Moddik removed the six or seven pointed rods from the chair, and began to stuff them in an extraordinary apparatus that appeared to be growing into a gray jelly at the center of the room.

"I could ask Danor," I said. "She was in my circle. But then, he may not have been in my circle." As I said this, the pulse in my throat slammed me so hard I had to swallow to get rid of it. "He, oh, he said he got the body at BAA, via BEE. I suppose he reckoned that way, even if BEE got suspicious, they'd never catch up to him in time."

"Bright lad," said Moddik. "I shall look forward to meeting him. My prefab horror should be arriving, courtesy of the Committee, about noon," he added, "I gave them directions, so it won't land on the fire-root or anything. Then I'll want that extra machine I mentioned from the ship—and, with any luck, by sunset tonight, the first water mixer will be serviceable. Not as beauteous as our friend out there, just ropy old steel nozzles and an ice-glass dome, but it'll water the land, and that's the idea, isn't it?"

"What can I say?" I asked him. "I'm overwhelmed."

"Then go and investigate your double and leave me in peace, you wretch of a Jang girl," roared Moddik, flapping sleeves and steel tubing and an unseen, nonexistent, ancient sorcerer's white beard.

"Hallo, *ooma*, may I join in?" Danor asked, gliding into the saloon from which Yay and Jaska were clearing the messy remains of the Jang's dawn meal. I was eating the home-grown sun-peaches for mine. I handed her the dish, with slight misgiving.

"They're lovely, and they seem OK, but are you sure you want to? I may start an indiscriminate hair growth or something."

"Might be pretty," said Danor. "Long flamy gold-brown hair growing out, um, everywhere."

We giggled secretively in the way of females who have shared many and varying experiences together. Having been in the same circle did count for something, despite my constant propaganda to the contrary.

"Oh, well, anyhow, that smashing nut Moddik was in here last night gobbling those pink things, so I reckon we might all just as well get boils together."

We gnawed in silence awhile. Presently, pouring us fire-and-ice, I told her about the advent of Esten, what he had said, what Moddik had said, quite a lot about my own feelings on the subject.

Danor looked taken aback. I hadn't, selfish and feeble-minded that I am, thought of the implications for her conforted by another me-as-male, a duplicate of the one with whom she had whiled away the hours without Kam. But, in point of fact, this scarcely seemed to trouble her, and she received my awkward mutterings calmly.

"No, *ooma*," she said, "I was just considering what Moddik said, how it might be someone you know. I haven't met him yet, but—do you remember what I told you about our circle when I got here?"

"Yes," I said, and elegantly held up my hand (his gesture —my gesture—I'd caught it back off him). "Honestly, I did think of that. But, how would he ever dare?"

"Oh, I don't think daring it would be the problem," said Danor.

Hergal, female, with a male like my previous body, going off to BAA . . . I looked into my wine and didn't say it. I truly didn't know what I should say, or think. Or do.

Not, of course, that really I could do anything.

10

The unit passed, though "passed" is hardly the word for it. It seemed to me the whole organized (?) structure of the community was going to pot. Or, at any rate, there were now only Yay and me out there hoeing, tying things up, earmarking things for extra water, and also—food task—pruning the vines and fruit trees and getting quick-growing fern to go south, south, dammit, and get off the tubers. Borss meanwhile had somehow become Moddik's assistant in the workshop, which I could hardly resent (I told myself resentfully) since they were water-mixer making, a deed due to be for the general good.

However, other members of the general good . . .

Danor and Kam were over in the western area of the Garden. Moddik had said he thought he'd seen some *gerkalli* fruits, or something equally unlikely-sounding, coming up there. We'd gone to look, and sure enough *gerkalli* fruits they were, apparently. Kam had offered to stay and weed them out—desert weed is very nice, and can be directed into a grand display at the edges of the irrigation canals and thereby off the crops, since luckily it prefers hanging over water to strangling things. Kam and Danor also planned to extend one of the canals to join up with another, so I gave them Jaska and my blessing, thinking how worthwhile they were for helping and working so spontaneously. Back on my own with Yay, though, I had to keep pushing stupid "I-am-solitary-and-fed-up" thoughts from my mind. My cursing was a pleasure to hear. If any one had.

Naz lay on the veranda in permanent ecstasy, smiling at the green branches above. The swan lay in the green branches, smiling down at Naz. Esten's dragon, which was going to be a drag, had been tethered at the edge of a clearing after it had torn up a young tree and bitten it in pieces with innocent cries of delight.

Nilla was making Her Own Garden. Moddik had suggested it, presumably to occupy her nonexistent mind. She

was appropriating flowers and replanting them in Her Own
Garden, where fortunately they took philosophical root.
They were, without exception, pink flowers, like Nilla, with
her magnolia skin and dusky strawberry hair, and she was
making, for a centerpiece a Jang abstract sculpture out of
bits of Moddik's leftover ice-glass. Which was all going to
be, of course, astoundingly useful.

Moddik's expected materials arrived at noon, as he'd said.
He'd somehow persuaded the Q-R set-up to use the displacer to get them through quickly. Crates of atrocious, incomprehensible metal objects and plastic slabs therefore exploded
into being in the clearing, and scared Esten's dragon into rip-
ping up another tree. Moddik checked them himself to save
me the trouble.

The rest of the party were located thus: Glis and Felain in
secret in the yellow cabin. Passing the door once, there seemed
to be some sort of poetry and music recital going on
rather than what one would have expected. Talsi, meanwhile,
was being brazenly wanton out among the groves with Phy and
Loxi. From their direction—roughtly due south—climactic
screams came with monotonous regularity.

As for Esten, he had been invited into Talsi's grove and
graciously declined; he had been invited into Glis and Felain's
cabin and had declined even more graciously. Nilla had
tried to lure him into Her Own Garden, but he had sensibly
said he felt exhausted and was going to sleep for ten hours.
I'd tried to keep out of his way, mostly because I'd rather
have plonked myself right next to him.

"Take the green cabin," I said. "It's the last one free, and
you may have to share with Naz, if he ever comes around
enough to get there."

Before Esten vanished to slumber, however, I'd seen him in
conversation with Moddik at the workshop door. Very earn-
est they both looked. Was Moddik explaining the inter-valvu-
lar pump circuits or something?

I stamped about in the greenery in a furious state of complete irrationality, and uncovered, during the course of the
afternoon, four sets of Gray-Eyeses having it off, a snake
making a hole and digging up one of the anti-earth-tremor
stabilizers I'd so laboriously put down, and a new mauve
animal swimming in an irrigation canal, which took one look
at me and fled wailing into the undergrowth. Gradually many
new types of this and that were wandering in. A sand-rabbit
or two bounced through the fern, and dune-frogs croaked

messages to each other through the desert nights. The insects were acquiring most *derisann* extra colors on their tinsel wings, and very *groshing* they looked. I passed from wonder to annoyance and back twenty times, and it was sunset, all at once, before I was ready.

Moddik showed us the water mixer at sunset, his eyes brilliantly alert as the shiny little wheels that spun in the mixer's dome.

It wasn't lovely to look at, as he'd predicted it wouldn't be. Rather shorter than the original striding giant of whipped cream and mother-of-pearl, its semi-opaque ice-glass dome looked slightly indecent. Its squat body, mounted on tall yet somehow squat metal legs, had a freakish demoniac appearance. But when he touched the activator, the water misted from it like a sweet dream.

It went bumbling off purposefully, just as the original stalking colossus returned. They passed each other, stepping imperiously over the smaller trees, and looking like a beautiful maker and her ugly child who, differences unresolvable, refused to speak to each other.

I thanked Moddik lavishly. The Jang were impressed.

Nilla said, "How *drumdiky* it looks. Not decorative at all. Makes me positively *tosky*," trying to inspire Moddik to maul her. She was wearing her most unembroidered see-through and had been picking the flowers again to adorn her hair. Moddik patted her on the head with a wicked look of senile indulgence, and Nilla fumed.

We were going off to sixth or seventh meal, but Moddik said he'd had a meal injection and wouldn't bother.

"And I can easily get through the night on some stay-awake pills, my dear young leader, and present you with eight or nine undecorative but useful water mixers come the dawn. Now I have the mold, it's just a production line in here."

"Stay-awake pills," I said. "Meal injections."

"You mustn't think Jang have the monopoly on misuse of the body," he reproved me. "Never fear, I shall snore the whole unit away tomorrow."

"How disappointing for Nilla."

The Jang were riotous in the saloon. Why not?

Danor and Kam, tired by honest toil, as I was, talked quietly with me. Naz floated above our heads on a float-cushion. Where was he getting so much ecstasy from? Moddik must have given it to him to keep him quiet. Loxi sidled over and invited me to the never-ending Talsi orgy, and I said something vile enough to send the entire menage hurrying off to their float-beds.

I went along the corridor with soil-burned feet and a spiteful mien.

Yellow cabin: Felain and Glis, no music now.

Apricot cabin: Loxiandphy, plus Talsi. It sounded like battle in there, what on earth—? Oh, *graks* to it.

Violet cabin: Danor and Kam. Controlling of foul thoughts. Sleep well, or whatever you're up to, nice people.

Scarlet cabin: Nilla, who else? Pink Nilla on scarlet bed, pink hair spread on scarlet pillow. Nilla constructing a plan of action—how to get Moddik. Rotten dreams, *ooma,* and if you pick any more of those flowers I'll bury you up to your neck in Gray-Eyeses' natural fertilizer.

Green cabin: Esten stretched out for ten hours sleep.

Estenmyself.

The poet's body, slender steel in a marble glove. Limber and strong as whipcord, didn't I just know? Shadowy eyes, shut, lashes like black fringes of needles. White plains, dark valleys, hair line curling fern . . . Damn, damn, and damn.

Well? Why not go in? So you lost mind, soul, and heart to me, eh? Here I am. Show me.

Hergal, I said, almost aloud. Just the kind of mean, tantalizing game you'd play on me. Give me so much on a plate you know I'd never take it, then leave it all up to me to come crawling back.

Yet, so clever to make yourself me, to sound even rather like me, certainly not really like you, Hergal, my friend, my lover, whom I knocked right through that wall in Four BEE, thereby beginning the end.

I'd gone past. I'd reached my own cabin, the blue one.

I went through the open door alone, and shut it.

11

The subtle muted cabin lights didn't come on. Some other mess-up in my far-from-perfect ship. The malfunction didn't seem dangerous, though. I'd see to it in the morning.

There were no lights in the bathing unit either, but the scented water worked, and warm air and towels jumped on me out of the wall with their usual terrifying alacrity.

It was very dark, only faint starlight smokily seeping in at the window through blue gauze—I'd forgotten to draw the curtain open, which was odd, for I thought I had. Maybe my poor little overtaxed mind was giving out.

I found the bed, not too easily, tired and bemused as I was, banging my unclothed anatomy on furniture, and uttering oaths resplendent in their inventiveness and squalor.

I sank on to the bed, head and body singing like slackened strings. And at once hands had me, turned me. I was gripped and held, firmly yet unbruisingly, close as the earth holds what grows from it, all the length of a male body.

I knew it at once. How not. It had been mine.

The contact was so vital, so instantaneous, so predictably electric, I could no more have thrust him off than I could resist some painless, potent anesthetic gas.

Skin on skin. He was naked as I was. He didn't caress me or speak to me, simply held me there, letting my flesh find him out, even if my brain refused to do so.

But my brain, submerged, overwhelmed by my flesh, remembered and, remembering, conjured him from itself till we seemed one thing, indivisible. He understood my compliance before ever I put my arms around him, before ever I said:

"Tell me who you really are."

"You," he said into my mouth—his mouth, my mouth. "Who else?"

Later, he was laughing at me. I could see him laugh, for one small light—he'd asked Moddik how to fix the lights—

had been allowed to come on. His eyes were sapphire in that dark glow, as my eyes must be too, for my eyes were still the poet's eyes, Esten's eyes. Those eyes would make us look, though all else was different, like children of one maker, one womb.

"Well now," he said, "was I as good as you were when you were me?"

12

Dawn pierced golden-green through the forest leaves, the glacia-view, the blue gauze, and woke us.

"Dearest *ooma*," he said, "what's that racket?"

"Frogs? Binni-thing-a-mies? What racket? My heart, perhaps, stirred by your nearness."

"Or mine by yours? No. A kind of humming."

"Nilla in the bath unit?"

"Fool of my dreams. A metallic sound. Robots?"

"Yay in the bath unit? He'll go rusty."

"Do you always get this silly after love?" he asked me.

"Don't you know, *ooma?*"

"Still striving to guess my identity when I tell you we've never met before?"

"Still striving. I'll guess. Maybe I have."

"I don't think so," he said, seriously, with that heart-wrenching, loin-quickening sorrow chiseling his handsome face just as it had once chiseled my handsome face. "You see, whatever else, you're bound to be confused by the subconscious permanent notion that I'm really you. It diverts and tangles you up, doesn't it?"

"Yes. I think it's sick and perverted, and we're a couple of perverts, you to think of it, me to agree to it. And don't go on looking at me like that or I'll demand further proof of how much I like it, and you're obviously far too fragile to cope with so much libido, what with your consumption and all."

"Balls," said my lover.

"Quite," I said, and got off the bed.

I could hear it now, that humming, very clearly.

I stared through the window, but sun and leaves and the ravages of lust made seeing out difficult.

"I'm going to investigate," I said.

"You always were a nosy character."

"Whoops," I said. " 'Always were.' Your former relationship with me is showing."

153

We weren't outside for another hour, of course. When we made it, both pairs of sapphire-opal eyes with romantic rings under them, the terrace was alive. Everyone was out, and first meal was being eaten.

Danor glanced up at us, and never smiled. Or rather, her whole body smiled, everything absolutely beaming approval, everything but her mouth, which she very carefully kept straight. Kam, on the other hand, grinned broadly, and said something under his breath that sounded like "Cheers."

The Jang were too preoccupied with being Jang really to notice; only Nilla shot us an evil look, and Esten bowed to her.

Then a warm, murmurous voice sounded in my ear, and surprised me: Talsi.

"Moddik has asked us to meet him, just beyond the purple trees, as soon as possible."

"Do you mean to say he's really made nine water mixers?" I asked.

Talsi said, "Very definitely. I think the dear creature wants to show them off."

"Why not?" I cried, grabbing up a fruit from the table—everyone seemed to be eating them now, bar Nilla. Even Naz had a sun-peach, but he was probably too blasted to realize what it was, maybe thought it was a syntho-cake or something.

"Come on," I said. "Let's go and see Moddik's water mixers."

The Jang groaned and prised themselves off the angelfood. One good thing, when the provision dispenser had to switch onto pure syntho-basics there'd be no more of that yuk served up on my ship.

Esten, Danor, Kam, and I went first, the Jang tottering after. Glis and Felain had even persuaded Naz into coming. Talsi came last, rather as if shepherding us. Her maternal sex-drive thing again?

We'd forgotten about the humming, Esten and I, and got used to it meanwhile. Now I recollected, because right here was the source.

"Good day," said Moddik, as we emerged on the grass lawn just beyond the grove, and found ourselves facing a semicircle of water mixers.

"Moddik!" I exclaimed. "There are twelve! Do they all work?"

"Of course. Do you doubt the master?"

"Activate them," I pleaded. "Let's get soaked with mixed-water rain. Or shall I press the starter?"

Moddik stared at me, and suddenly he wasn't the same. He looked portentous, somehow. Maybe his achievement had moved him.

"A moment," he said. "Before we do anything, I'd like everybody to listen to something I have to say."

Not one of us missed it. A sort of change in the air, like the change you finally come to recognize in the atmosphere before a sandstorm or before the great rains. In the absolute quiet I said:

"Moddik, has something grim happened? If it has, could you tell us quickly? Because perhaps every second counts."

"Nothing grim," said Moddik. "It may seem so, just for a split. But if we take it calmly, I think we can work it out."

I was so tense, I jumped when Esten spoke.

"Do the water mixers actually work?"

"Oh, yes. They really are water mixers. Have you already guessed, Jang Esten, what I've been up to?"

"No. I'm not certain. You'd better tell us, anyhow."

"Yes, you'd better," said Kam from my right, "and fairly fast."

13

That expression on Moddik's face had an unpleasant familiarity. I couldn't think what it reminded me of. He said:

"Here it is, then. In a nutshell, so to speak. The Committee in Four BEE has no personal grudge against any of you, contrary to what you rather egotistically surmise. The cause for their alarm is only that you may damage yourselves in some irreparable emotional fashion, and others also in more widespread and terrible ways. You are, though you may not properly comprehend the term, anarchists. As such, particularly considering the comparative strength of your numbers —or the strength which your members may eventually attain, since so many in the cities appear to sympathize and lean toward your mode of existence and your ideals—as such, I repeat, you are very, very dangerous. For your own sake and for the sake of those who may misguidedly follow you, you are asked to surrender to us, here and now, and return voluntarily to PD. No harm is offered you. Ultimately, we are acting in your own interests."

"We?" I said. I'm not sure how I managed to say anything. "We?"

"I myself, Talsi, Glis," he said. Talsi and Glis slipped out of our group and to his side. Then I recollected where I'd seen that look before. The Committee Hall.

"You're Q-Rs—you're androids," I said.

Nilla screamed. Even in our extremity, I thought how typical of her that was.

"I thought you were too good to be true," said Esten, "but I couldn't work it out in time."

"You were too intent on the seduction of your leader," said Moddik.

"Yes," I said, "and I on him. And Danor and Kam intent on each other and those fruits you so conveniently found over westward. And Nilla and her garden. And Felain wrapped up with Glis, and Loxi and Phy with Talsi. And Naz ecstasied up to his eyes. Beautifully staged, android. Just

156

derisann, you Q-R turd. I should have got on to you earlier,
shouldn't I? Sampling that fruit in the saloon—so human of
you, or were you testing it to see if we really could live on
them? And that crap about stay-awake pills. You've never
needed sleep in your short tubing-and-dial life. Oh, it's too
classic for words. Your plane even crashed, didn't it? To make
sure I wouldn't turn you away? I'm aghast at your splendid
acting. And so clever in overriding my block on the robots—I
wondered how you did that. I wondered how you got the
monitor computer to do exactly what you said, as well. I
know now, don't I? And all that pseudo-history you and those
two there flashed about, your Jang circle two *rorls* back . . .
you even knew Assule, of course, and said what a clot he was
because you understood how I'd love it. How well they must
have *programmed* you. Hey, Glis, you were right on, weren't
you? He really *can* understand the brain of a machine. He
should, and so should you. You're bloody *all* machines."

"Not quite," he said to me. "No life spark is required to
create an android, since we are electronically motivated,
but we are grown from cells and possess flesh as you do.
Even if a few superior mechanisms do go into our life
support. For example, Exile Jang, if I wished, I could pick up
your sand-ship and carry it out across the dunes. Let me see
you do it, life-spark human."

I felt sick, partly because I'd liked him, trusted him, admired him. But also because it was finally out, the bare facts
of their rivalry, what I had always instinctively felt. Programmed they might be to serve human needs, but in some
hidden dark of their personae, they hated and despised us.
Give them an excuse for retaliation, and they'd turn it on us
like a gun. Dear God, what now?

"So what have you done, super-android?" I asked softly.
"There's got to be some threat hanging over us, hasn't there?
You know we wouldn't buy your offer otherwise."

"He's rigged something," Esten said. "The water mixers,
probably."

"No reason for you to hazard," said Moddik and Q-R. "I'm
going to tell you. It *is* the water mixers, also my workshop
behind us by the grove of trees, also your robot Borss, currently in the sand-ship, also—must I enumerate further? I
put the materials the Committee sent me to good use. The
water mixers are particularly nice—real water-mixers that
really work, except that at the moment they are mixing
something else. Such a touch amused me. You see, we are

capable of humor. A moment's rewiring would alter them to their original purpose, of course, but none of you, I think, will be in a position to see to that."

"Don't dress it up," said Kam. His voice was as soft as mine had been, as soft as Esten's voice—as if we were similarly afraid to speak normally in case it precipitated the catastrophe. *"What's* in the water mixers, the workshop, the robot—and everywhere else you've put your hands?"

"Bombs," said the Q-R. "Each on its own big enough to throw this small area sky-high, and higher. Together, quite a pyrotechnic display. Very little is going to be left of your plantation, or your ship. Or, my human friends, of you. Even if you start running now, you won't outstrip the blast, and believe me the perimeter of such a shock is worse than the center."

"He's lying," said Kam. "You're lying. Activate, and you go, too. Don't you?"

"Just so," said the Q-R, "but I have no—er—soul. This thing that upsets you so much, this thing you call 'death,' is nothing to me. I shall have aided the Committee and mankind at large. The planes from Limbo will collect your remains and you will enter PD as planned. Everything will be as it should be."

"Wait," I said. "You can't harm humanity, can you? Or did your programming slip?"

"Oh, no," he said smiling. "I could plant the bombs, yes, since in their nonactive state they are harmless, and forever would be. I could not, however, depress a switch that would result in loss of human life—murder. But you see in Four BEE I was serviced in a slapdash fashion, deliberately, so that ultimately, at a moment that could be computed precisely, I should malfunction. And it is my malfunction which will activate the bombs, by means of the normal, upper-tonal malfunction alarm signals emitted from my inner circuitry. Do you understand? It's rather neat. The Committee are responsible only for the error in my servicing, not for the bombs. I am responsible for placing the bombs, not for my malfunction. The right hand does not know what the left hand does, so neither hand is guilty. Two parts of a whole, independent of each other, yet they act perfectly as one. But I digress. Maybe I should explain that the moment of my malfunction is several splits in the past, and the signals are already being issued. It will take exactly twelve splits more for them to penetrate the casings of the explosive and trigger the vital

nerve. After which there will be something of a bang." He
looked at me; his eyes danced, glinted, danced. "If all of you
make a run for it, the Jang bird-plane in the grove of trees behind you will get you clear in time, even overloaded though
the vehicle will be. I must point out, though, that its controls
are set for Four BEE Limbo. The setting, by the way, is ir-
reversible."

"If we agreed to go," said Kam abruptly, "you'd stop the
signals, stop these bombs going off?"

"I myself have no power to stop my own signal emission. I
would need to be dismantled."

Nilla screamed again.

"I'll go," she screeched. "I don't want to be hurt," and she
fled toward the grove and the plane.

"Yes," said Esten. "We'll all leave, won't we? But look," he
went toward the Q-R anxiously. "I left some stuff in the ship.
Could I just go and get it before—"

"It happened too fast for me. Esten flung himself into
Moddik. Too fast for Moddik as well. An android is physically constructed like a human, at least externally, so the fist
that went into his thorax upset the lung and heart mechanism, and the other fist that cracked on the jaw jarred those
hard bones just enough to black-out, momentarily, the steel
brain that whirred inside the plastic skull. Moddik fell,
crashed full length, and, as he did so, Talsi and Glis fell
also. Esten crouched over the Q-R, his face wild, desperate
and gray-pale through the desert tan.

"In his workshop," he shouted to me. "Electronic knives
—a pane of ice-glass—anything sharp—"

I ran. I'd never run so fast on legs made entirely of luke-
warm water. The workshop shelter was a confusion of bits
and pieces. I grabbed a molecule-needle knife and ran out
again.

"Here," I dived down beside Esten, then turned my head,
not ready for the thing he did with the knife, the spurt of
completely human-looking blood.

"This is going to be messy," he said, looking sicker than
me, but more in control of himself.

"Do you know what you're doing?" I blurted.

I could hear Nilla and Felain screaming from the back-
ground. The others just stared.

"Partly," he said. "I read it up, android and robot basics—
History Tower. I had an idea they might try something
like this—but not yet—not so soon—"

"What can I do?"

"Get one of the robots. We need some kind of liquid spray —water, oil, anything, just to wash this damned red metallic plasma out. I've got to cut through every single nontissue organ to stop that signal."

I got up and around again, but Kam said, "I'll do it," and ran, as I had, toward the forest area where the robots were hoeing.

Esten's hands gnawed on the corpse. Glis and Talsi lay as if dead. Moddik was definitely finished, and, extensions of him, the two "women" had presumably stopped like chronometers once he ceased to be.

Kam sprinted back, the robots clanking after.

"OK," Esten said, "now I handle it. The rest of you get out, and take those screaming fools with you."

"We stay," said Kam. "We can't miss it if it goes off, anyway."

"You might. Get as far away from the ship as you can, and climb down into one of those irrigation canals when it's due. Take a breath and lie on your faces under the water and stay put. It might work. Now do it, for God's sake."

The knife sizzled and spat through liquid, more slowly through steel fibers and hard plasti-rubber. The engines of android life lay spasmodically bare between the rushes of plasma and the squirting oil sprays of Jaska and Yay. It was a somber golden oil. When it met the "blood" it turned the color of Moddik's garnet hair.

"Go *on*," Esten raged coldly, not looking at us. "You've got about three splits."

"All right," Kam said.

I felt but did not see them moving, going swiftly to do what he said. Nilla and Felain were taken too, wailing. Loxi had started wailing as well. Would they be able to get the swan down from the roof, or wherever it was? What about the Gray-Eyeses? What about—?

"You too, you bitch," Esten said. I hadn't made a sound, but he knew I wasn't gone. I don't know why I wasn't. I was half-dead of fright. I wanted to run screaming like the Jang girls, run and not stop. But somehow I felt safer there, standing behind him.

"I'd—" I said, but he cut in as if he hated me.

"Push off. I'm trying to save your shitting land and your stupid hide. Let me *do* it."

So I did what he said. I ran. But not very far. There was

a channel quite close—too close, but I couldn't seem to reason it out, and half fell down into it. The water was very shallow, barely reached my ankles. I lay in it, attempting to pull the water up over myself.

I was crying in dry throaty gasps, and trying to count.

But I wasn't counting. I was praying. Like once before. A sort of prayer. Although nobody had answered that one. "No, please no, don't let it—Oh please no oh no oh no—"

It wasn't quiet. There were lots of noises. Animals, breezes through reeds and flowers and leaves. As if everyone were speaking for the last time, hurrying to get out its song of life before the blast tore it in shreds.

Then I heard someone shriek, off to the west. Nilla, maybe. Was it time, and did they know over there?

Now it happens.

Now it comes.

The red wind, the black sound.

Pain and silence forever.

I don't *want* to die. I'm not ready. None of us are ready. I don't want *this* to die, all this around me. I *want* the ache in my muscles from a day's work, I want the ache in my heart from anger or despair. I want every misery and joy I've ever known, and the rest to come. I want them all. They're all precious. And the trees, and the earth, and the sky . . .

Why doesn't it happen? I've bitten through the skin of my hand. Do I have to start on the other hand? It's going to, so let it be now.

Nothing
Happened
At
All.

Kam was hauling me up the bank of the canal, through the pretty weed.

"Kam, are we dead?"

"No," he said, quite reasonably, as if I'd said something intelligent and unusual that deserved a thinking man's answer. "We're OK. It didn't happen. Felain had a chronometer—Glis' chronometer, ironically enough—and I time-checked. Fifteen splits now since it should have happened. All clear."

"Then where's Esten?" I sprang up covered in mud, weed, the complete detritus my position had offered me, and hurled myself past the purple trees, onto the lawn.

Tanith Lee

Or practically.

He was still there by the Q-R corpse, the knife silent and immobile in his hand. He looked exhausted, literally shattered, as if some framework in him had given way. But then, was that yet another complication of the poet-body syndrome?

"Esten—" I called out, and he shouted:

"Wait—stay back."

"But it's finished," I said. "Fifteen splits since it should—"

"I got them all," he said, "all but one. I got that too, when I found it, but I was over the time. It could be safe. It may not be. Something may still—" he broke off, staring at me, then cried at the top of his lungs: "Down, get *down!*"

Kam was behind me, and pushed me. We fell like desperate lovers together into the grass and the green land smashed us, rising.

The noise was like no-noise, a bang so big it went beyond sound into a sort of clap of deafness.

The sky rained fire and debris. Leaves fell in masses and covered us.

Presently, it was over.

It had only been one water mixer, the seventh and farthest from us at the center of the semicircle. Esten had cut all the signals in time but the last; that last went on long enough to eat through the bomb casing and then peter out. The nerve of the bomb flickered, hesitated, wondering if it were detonated or not. It wondered for fifteen splits. Then decided it was, and blew.

Smoke was clearing in snatches.

I wasn't hurt, but so divorced from myself I could only crawl on my hands and knees. Kam, also unhurt, muttered after me, but I took no notice.

I got to Esten quickly, even that way. I thought he was going to be dead, but I still had to get to him.

He wasn't dead. He was breathing and simply looked like a beautiful poet passed out on some romantic lawn. That was from his left side. When I went around to the other side, the side the blast had been, I saw that he was never going to be beautiful, never going to look as I had looked, ever again.

14

I knew very well what the answer would be, but I had to try. I tried for hours, for days. I tried shouting, pleading, speaking extremely serenely and rationally. I wept and I swore.

The computer simply reiterated its message. We were to use the painkilling drugs we possessed, the antibiodermics, the healing salve. Further supplies would be sent us.

"The salve isn't good enough," I kept saying. "It can't heal that kind of wound—not properly."

The computer said that pain could be alleviated, and infection prevented, that this was the most that we were entitled to, exiles as we were. We knew that new bodies were no longer allowed us, or any form of surgery or replacement.

"But the skin is—the scar will be—"

Rattle click. Rattle click.

Click.

"Damn you," I screamed, "It's your fault!"

Rattle, rattle.

"Your bloody fault—your plot—it didn't come off! Your stinking Q-Rs are melted all over the grass out there—"

Kam shut off the link before I could elaborate.

"No use," he said. "It's on Receive Only. You won't get any more reaction."

"Whatever they send—drugs, supplies—how can we trust them?"

"We'll check everything they send," he said, "as you suggested earlier. But I don't think they'll try again. That point about their programming still holds good—they could only go as far as they did by blinding themselves to it. It's out in the open now. Next time they *would* know. Ergo, they won't."

"Oh, what does it matter, anyway?"

There was a great stillness in the ship. They were mostly sitting in the saloon. Nilla and Felain were intermittently crying, but very softly, holding on to each other for dear life. Naz was generally pacing in the corridor; each time he turned at either end the Jang topaz beads on his trouser hems came together with a little cold clink. We had been going on like this, with minor variations, for five units.

I opened the door of my cabin.

Danor was sitting with him. She was quite motionless, and so was he, but he was at last awake.

I'd been hoping he wouldn't wake up for an indefinite while, though, of course, there wasn't any pain, not with the miraculous drugs, so easy to use and so expedient. The whole of the right side of his face and neck was shielded by a silk-of-ice bandaging, under that the anesthetic foam barrier, keeping the material from actually touching the ruined flesh. The blast had ripped the side of his face open, peeling back the tissues in layers—somehow, incredibly, it had missed the mouth, the nostril, the eye. So it was with two eyes, those eyes that were still mine, that he was able to look up at me as I came toward him.

"Hello, Esten," I said.

"Hello," he said.

The right eardrum had been badly damaged, but that didn't necessarily have to matter. The robots and the machines had already worked out and implanted some sort of miniaturized something or other that would do the ear's work for it—a process they knew, since it was part of their own self-servicing technique.

Danor rose and went out. I didn't want her to go. I didn't want the responsibility of being alone with him, conscious. Unconscious, I had sat by him here four days, four nights, barring my sessions with the monitor computer, when Kam or Danor relieved me.

I'd felt helpless enough then, useless enough. But now.

I didn't know what I could say to him. Particularly since—

"Sit down," he said courteously. "I suggest that we should talk."

"Do you feel up to talking? I think—"

"I think you'd rather not talk, and you're putting the onus on me. But I say we have to, and I'm fine, so pull up a float-chair and sit down."

"Very well."

I sat, and I peered at him. I wanted to cry. He said:

"You don't bravely have to stare me out, you know." So I lowered my stinging eyes, ashamed.

"I look fairly grizzly, I imagine," he said calmly, "and when this excellent bandaging comes off, I'm going to look sixteen times worse. Aren't I?"

"Not necessarily. You see, the salve is still very good. And if you keep on using it—it may take a while, but—"

"Shut up, *ooma*," he said. "You never could lie about anything that really mattered to you. Just listen to me, and then we'll have it straight. I came out to this place to get you, and I got you, and I don't regret it. Neither do I regret saving your greenery from extinction. However, I do see that as your bed mate, with this face, my days are numbered. So, in a little while, Naz is going to bring me in his total hoard of renounced ecstasy and a few other things as well, and I'm going blissfully to overdose myself out of this Ego-Life, into PD."

I jumped—off the chair, backward, upward—

"No," I shouted. "PD is out. Suicide is out. You'd give them the satisfaction of voluntarily doing what they tried to push us into—after *this?*"

"*Ooma*, it's my life, what's left of it. It's up to me."

"No, not any more it isn't."

"Please don't squeeze out a host of insincere protestations of eternal affection, or start howling that my irrevocable hideousness will make no difference to you. You'll only regret it, and I shan't swallow a syllable."

Somehow I'd got back to the chair, and flattened myself down in it as if an ogre were after me. Perhaps it was.

"Let me do what I want," he said. "There'll be other males along, you can be sure of that. Run a check to make sure they're human next time."

"Be quiet," I said. I tried to get my breath, and realized I wasn't going to be able to, so I'd have to explain it all to him without breath. "First, I *know* it makes a difference. What else could it do? Every time I look at that scar—oh, yes, there's going to be one bloody awful scar—my guts are going to knot up like a nest of reinforced steel cobras. Not with revulsion, with anger. Anger that it happened to you. What other difference could there be? You're still you—still *me*, you body-thieving bastard. If your hair went white, would I stop feeling anything for you? What does it matter anyway? In Four BEE and BAA and BOO the physical side was, in any case, a joke, wasn't it? If you fell for someone, you fell for *them*, their personality—their—their self, whatever it is—not whatever flesh they happened to have put on that unit. Which is why any true feeling was rare. Oh, yes, the body turned me on, looking like me and everything, but it's you who got through to me, you fool. And this thing that's happened to you—it's something that was *done* to you, not you yourself. You're still *you*." I managed to get a breath then, and I stabbed the last words out at him as a final cold blow to bring him back to his senses and to me. "Still you—*Hergal*."

"Oh," he said, quite lamely. He looked as if he might be going to laugh.

"Of course," I added, "maybe you're so effete you can't live with it yourself. Maybe you don't give a damn about me. You just want to piss off to nice PD and leave me here alone for the rest of my days with your filthy little child to bring up."

"What?" he said.

I caught up with myself just then.

"Er, I hadn't quite meant to tell you, like that. Oh, I'm not even absolutely sure. Actually. So, er. Yes."

"Well, I think you'd better tell me. Again. Quietly and in detail."

I rose, and then sat on the edge of the bed.

"You see," I mumbled, feeling acutely embarrassed for some reason I couldn't fathom, "Kam and I were near the bomb blast, so we ran checks on ourselves to be sure everything was still in order physically. And it was. But my machine had a little fit and spat out bits of blue tape over me, and it said I was—it's the old word—pregnant. That means that you and I have done what we wouldn't have been allowed to do in the cities, which is, make a child. Only instead of growing in the crystallize tanks, ever so hygienic and safe and everything, the poor little idiot's going to have to grow inside *me*. I'm carrying, fecund, in the club, um, etc. I couldn't work out why, to begin with, but the machine did eventually. It's the 'home-grown' food I've been devouring so rapaciously. Those tubers and sun-peaches and lettuce things. It *has* altered my body chemistry, screwed up the contraceptive properties that apparently linger in our exclusive city diet. So, whoops, we're going to be makers, Hergal, and if you go off and leave me here, I'll never forgive you."

He just lay there, expressionless. I wondered if he'd grasped what I'd said; I could hardly grasp it myself. Then he took my hand, and he said:

"If you want me to stay, I'll stay. But there's one thing we'd better have clear from here on. I'm not Hergal."

I gazed at him, and wildly verbalized a list of males who at one era or another had been close: Drar? Rannik? *Lorun?*

"No," he said. He looked at me and then he told me.

And I didn't believe him.

"Twelve *vreks* back," he said, "that was the last time you ever really registered me, and not surprising. I couldn't express myself then, particularly not to you. You were like a wall of solid glowing metal. When I was with you, the heat and the brightness shriveled me up. I became all the things you hated most in sheer self-defense. I couldn't say a sentence to you that didn't sound as though it had come out of a rusty mincer. In the end, I instigated for myself a sort of game. I knew you expected me to be a dull, reactionary, clod-hopping lump, with a ragbag of platitudes in place of a brain— a kind of faithful *promok*, who'd dog your footsteps, and creep away when you got bored. Because I could never manage to put over my true thoughts against that glowing wall of indifference, I just used to act out the part you'd allotted me. I'd shamble up looking like Monster-Night, and say: '*Onk*, it's not ethical, but I mustn't grumble,' and blink a couple of my eyes at you, and I could see the circuits engaging in your mind, the right patterns being achieved. A sort of neon sign would light up in your face: Here comes that bloody silly cunt, Hatta. Of course, this was not the way to deal with you, but I'm a defensive man, oversensitive. I can't help it, I need a shell. I got a rather bitter and depressing laugh at the way you had me so wrong every time, and I played up to it. I could tell myself: She doesn't understand me because now I won't let her see me.

"Then they chucked you out of Four BEE, and that was it. I knew I'd got to come after you because you were the only thing that gave any value to my life. I'd been too nervous, too scared before to run on your road. The only time I'd ever put myself on the level, you'd smashed my ego down my throat. But out here there wasn't any other way. Being a monster freak has compensations, but not when there's nothing else you can be.

"To begin with, I had a spell of being female. I was trying to find out something about you, to get over the thing that scared me in you. And I succeeded. It was a kind of therapy I thought might work, and it did. Being a girl is not for me.

I'm eighty percent masculine, and stuck with it. But I found out what makes the clock tick, and high time. To nick your last male body was pure inspiration. Very disturbing it was, I might add. More for me, perhaps, than for you when you initially saw me. That was the first time, or almost the first time I'd ever had you at a disadvantage. No neon came up on this occasion. You were just completely nonplussed, standing out there in the glamorous remains of that jewelry dress, staring up at me. I'd tried to acquire your manner, your extrovert qualities, in order to deceive you. The strange thing is that I took to them quite easily, once I'd got over the fear of being in the open, not hiding behind six red eyes and eight legs."

His gaze never left my face while he said this. When he stopped, I said:

"Well, it looks rather as if the only one of us two who's a right *floop* is me."

He said, "Now you know who I am, do you still want me to stay?"

"Hatta—" I began, but he said:

"No, Esten. Let's keep that the way it is. Hatta is past tense."

"All right, Esten, then. You used to say, when you were Hatta the Horror, that you loved me."

"Unchanged," he said. "That's what it's about."

"Well—Esten—I don't know if I love you. But if you leave me, a bit of me will go with you. Maybe it's just the clever trick you devised, but you really do seem like a part of me, myself. And I've got your seed in me, growing, and I want that child, and I want you. What more can I say?"

"Knowing you," he said, "bloody plenty."

Epilogue

So we sit here on the veranda, Danor and I, like two fecund Gray-Eyeses. In our condition we're obviously too far gone to do much hoeing or digging. In fact I doubt if we could see over ourselves to the hoe.

Danor found out she too had doubled her ego-count some days after I did, but she didn't appear to mind. She looks sweetly lovely and positively scintillates with health, as I do. I suppose it's lucky for us the cities make such first-class body structures. Giving birth with only the knowledge you get from a machine and its library, and no experienced help beyond what a couple of pale and terrified males can offer, is a prospect not without its soul-destroying aspect, but I think we are perfectly built enough that we can cope, and anyhow we'll have to, pangs of cowardice or not. And who cares? It's going to be worth it.

"Mine will be male," says Danor. I surmise she wants to replace Kam's unloving child in BAA. But how can we know what sex our brats will be? A random life this is going to prove, all told.

We've had no more trouble from the cities, despite a sort of alarm system we arranged, to spot enemy planes and so forth. But so far, over the past *vrek* and a half, twenty new arrivals, each checked out as human, have appeared on the scene—only six of them females, which may create extra difficulties later, and I almost wish we had that android bitch Talsi around. They descend in stolen aircraft, stolen sky-boats . . . Three hijacked a sand-ship and five of the passengers elected to come with them when they saw the valley. They work very hard, though all at various things. We're starting to be able to recognize our own different talents, and channel them. For example, we have four terrific cooks, who can do wonders with the provision-dispenser goo (yes, we're on goo, and checked goo, at that) and even better wonders with the natural food. Fortunately others have robot and mechanic skills, not like Moddik, but then that's hardly surprising. With their help we've got a complete housing plan on the way, not to mention a reliable contraceptive for those girls who don't want to end up as Danor and I have done, while still enjoying the home-grown edibles. Plus a valley-wide discerning shock wall, almost complete, that discriminates between animals, humans, and *androids*.

Moddik's eleven remaining water mixers—safely rewired by clever Esten, who read about such things where I absorbed poetry in the History Tower—proudly prowl the Garden in the steps of that mother-of-pearl giant who came first. Except that they go much farther, to the edges of the dunes, in fact. Which is why the valley is green from rim to rim. Green, even over there, where the black crater left by Moddik's last bomb has healed with grass, like a symbol of all healing, of the body, the mind, the heart.

Sitting here, looking out across that landscape of small white homes, half built, the columns of trees, the different-colored lawns and slopes scattered with broken panes of shade and sun; smelling too the perfume that flows off the earth and the flowers, the city I came from seems unreal and forever silenced. Against the stature of those black mountains, against the vault of that blazing sky flashing back at itself like blue-green mirror from the canals, against the music of life, the animal cries, the insects, the din of humans working or arguing or making love or singing out there under the green shadows, it's not only Danor's womb and mine that seem quickened, but the whole defiant womb of our world.

Presently Nilla and Felain will be back from the carving they've started out there in the forest. These two at least won't need the contraceptive, being content with each other for the time being—to the great sorrow of several males. One artistic young man has already painted them as an Idyll. I think he's planning to have a go at Danor and me next as two pregnant tribal princesses. Hmm. Naz is raising some sort of corn over on the west side. He's very enthusiastic about it. Phy and Loxi are somewhere with two girls. In their spare moments they've commenced a hive for the insects, which apparently will make honey. (Sometime.) Esten's dragon has been harnessed to an old-fashioned robot-built plow, and doesn't like it too much. As for my inter-animal-android theories, the swan has been adopted by a family of snakes, and lives with them. Their fur makes it sneeze, but that doesn't seem to matter.

Kam will also be home soon. He'll put his arm around Danor as if she's marked HANDLE WITH EXTREME CAUTION, but she'll make him forget that later, in their cabin. Esten will be next, the color of mahogany, coming up from the forest. From the left he will look like a poet, or a young primitive deity out of the glades. From the right you will see the half-mask of polarized satin.

And when I think now how I almost quoted, not realizing, his own words of so long ago back at him, that day I made him stay alive with me—how the body was a joke, that it was the inner something which mattered . . . well, I've learned your new name, Esten, and I've learned that if I love anybody, yours is the name he gave himself.

Pet, do you hear it, my white pet, buried somewhere out there, over the mountains, under the sand? Do you hear the noise we're making?

The grapes should be harvested soon, and prepared in the ancient fashion. Perhaps I should send a flask of our vintage to Four BEE, with our compliments.

However nasty a drink it turns out, it's going to be better than their lousy sapphire wine.

Glossary of Conventions, Institutions, and Devices

android See Q-R.

bee (baa, boo) A kind of electronic, self-carrying "handbag" used by both sexes. It can contain anything from a bottle of wine to a full-length mirror; and will also run errands and carry messages. In Four BEE these things are known as bees, in Four BAA as baas, in Four BOO as boos.

body change and sex change The essential element—"life spark" or consciousness—can be taken from one body and replaced in another fresh body, specifically designed by the prospective occupant, via the Limbo Tub at Limbo. The chosen body may be either male or female, depending on the mood of the human concerned. In the earlier part of the autobiography the writer stated that the time supposed to elapse between each body replacement was officially thirty units, but this limit was constantly abused by suiciders.

circle Jang custom: A circle is a group of friends who more or less stick together as a clique, and are reckoned to do most things as one. Admitting fresh members to the circle is a complex ritual, although not mentioned by the writer. Cutting original members out, however, is easy, and the outcast is traditionally expected to dissolve in tears.

displacement machine Originally intended for human travel, on the disintegration-reintegration principle, it proved unpopular, since the process tended to make the passengers vomit—according to the writer.

Dream Rooms The place where citizens can buy and experience dreams previously designed and plotted by themselves—a kind of cerebral Adventure Palace.

flashes News bulletins, appearing as electrically projected signs in the sky, on walls, etc. They can also be picked up in

172

the home. Nothing much ever appears to happen in the cities, so anything even slightly unusual is worth reporting on, and zoom-scanners and Flash Center bees are constantly on the alert. There is a Flash Center in each of the four sectors of each of the cities.

Four BEE, Four BAA, Four BOO The three great dome cities. Obviously in size gargantuan, they exist beneath stabilized electricity wave shields—the domes—which protect them from all the hazards of the planet, eruption, storm, earthquake, and so on. Entirely self-sufficient, their inner conditions are made as "natural" as possible, complete with parks and gardens, days and nights, artificial sun, moon, and stars. Outside Four BAA are the lesser domes which contain the breeding-tank farms for the creation of Q-Rs and also glamorous android animals made to delight the populace. Four BOO is famous for the trapping of real desert animals—for pets—and additionally, in point of fact, for fur and other animal products such as scent.

hypno-school First active stage of city life, where children are taught incredibly sophisticated items, such as extraordinary forms of mathematics, for which apparently they never find any use afterward. Teaching by hypnosis leaves most of the school activity a complete blank in the child's mind, though knowledge is retained. This phase only lasts one-twentieth of a *rorl* (about five years).

Jang Second stage of city life. Adolescence has become a compulsory part of growing up, lasting anything up to half a *rorl* or longer, and is called Jang. Jang have their own customs, culture, traditional modes of behavior (having ecstasy, marriage, etc.), and virtually their own language (Jang slang). Any who depart from the norm are frowned on by all strata of society.

makers Parents. Relevant cells are taken from a male and a female who wish to become makers, and joined in a crystallize tank to make a child. This is supposed to create a bond between the two makers, but evidently rarely does for long. Only one maker is obliged to remain as the child's guardian, and then actually only until hypno-school is finished.

marriage Jang custom. Jang traditionally always marry before "having love"—the sexual act. Sometimes they marry for a substantial period of time—a *vrek*, mid-*vrek*, etc.—sometimes only for an afternoon or unit, in which case the marriage must be paid for both before and after. The marriage "ceremony" consists mainly of one speech, as follows: "I promise to have love with you and no other for the period aforesaid, unless I seek annulment, which may be granted on alternate units throughout the marriage, and which must be paid for." Older People are not required to marry.

Older People Final and longest stage of city life, which can continue more or less indefinitely, until the person concerned, worn out with living and memories, voluntarily seeks Personality Dissolution, in which his current ego is erased and his conscious mind washed clean of all recollection. After this he returns to the child stage once more, this time with a Q-R guardian.

paying There is no monetary system in Four BEE, etc. However, since the cities run on power, emotional energy is taken from the payer and fed into the city power banks. The weird process is accomplished simply by the purchaser entering a pay-booth and going into a hysteria of thank-yous. Ecstasy or other drug stimulants are generally used to ensure the success of this peculiar rite.

Picture-Vision A sort of nonstop TV extravaganza of beauty and eroticism, with no story line.

Q-R Quasi-robot, or android. Grown in the breeding tanks at BAA, from chemical cells, the Q-R externally resembles a human. Useful circuitry is built into them, however, and even their "blood" is a form of self-servicing metallic plasma. Not being created from male and female tissue and therefore without a consciousness—or life spark—the Q-Rs are brought to life by an electric charge of colossal force.

sabotage Is carried out by Jang, and is another, though unofficial, Jang custom. It entails breaking into the lookout posts of the cities, damaging the machinery, and thereby disturbing the protective waves of the dome long enough to allow in bad weather, or worse. The dome defenses quickly block the sabotage, and harm of any telling proportion is never done.

suiciding Literally suiciding—killing the body—but without the normal connotations, since it is only a means to get an off-the-cuff body replacement inside the thirty-unit limit. Limbo robots immediately home in on any suicide or death, and take the "victim" to Limbo, where they rescue the life spark and replace it in flesh.